THE PAPAYA KING

Also by Adam Pelzman

Troika

THE PAPAYA KING

ADAM PELZMAN

JACKSON HEIGHTS PRESS
NEW YORK

ISBN 978-1-7332585-3-1 (paper)
ISBN 978-1-7332585-1-7 (e-book)

Library of Congress Control Number: 2019908983

Cover design by Andrea Ho

For Ramona

One

🌊

Oh, what a lovely day it is! How intoxicated I feel, how inspired, as if the very Titans have united and imbued my troubled soul with all of their great powers. I am in fact bursting with such optimism, such benevolence, that if an acquaintance were to encounter me on the street today, he would no doubt stop and say, "Robert Walser, is that *you*? There's something different about you, as if you have become a god among men."

As I walk down 72nd Street from my apartment building, my gait is bouncy and confident. Behind me is the Hudson River, which despite the spectacular sky is an awful battleship grey. I take no more than ten strides on the far side of West End Avenue and reach the door of a baffling restaurant that never seems to be open when a restaurant should be open. The owner of this restaurant—one Stavros—waves from behind the plate glass window. I turn around to see if he is waving at me. (He is.) I smile and wave back to this man with a certain pity, as if I am bidding farewell to a prisoner being led off to the firing squad. The situation is almost that grave for Stavros, although he is blissfully unaware.

I want to ask why his establishment is closed between the hours of eleven in the morning and two in the afternoon, but he flashes me a grin suggesting such incomprehensible idiocy that I do not have the heart to confront him. I have learned many things over my thirty-two years, but perhaps the most useful is the importance of self-restraint. I can only imagine that to suggest to Stavros a more traditional operating schedule (being open for lunch, perhaps) would elicit in him not the gratitude that would be expected of most men, but rather a bemused chuckle suggesting that I am the one who lacks comprehension, not he.

"Mr. Walser," he might say, "Why don't you stick to writing those silly words, or whatever it is you do, and leave the commerce to me." And then, to prove his mastery over me, he would return to the counter and arrange with great precision the Linzer tortes, the bear claws, and the delicious apple turnovers as if he were setting a table for the King of France. I have accepted the fact that there is simply no way to convince such a man of his wrongness, for he—like the mule or the ox—is stubborn and self-righteous. So, it is best for me to leave him to his pastries and his empty restaurant and whatever sad and tragic fate awaits him.

As I continue my journey along 72nd Street, passing a cluster of small stores, I feel something on my shoulders, something ethereal and therapeutic that sneaks up on me from the west. A familiar yet rare sensation it is, for here comes the most soothing breeze, a warm and swaddling zephyr with a delightful ripple of autumnal promise, one that slides over the dreadful, white-capped river and bathes me on this most exquisite day. I wonder if it is possible for a man and a day to be so blessed—and I think this, *feel* this, because it was just this morning that I received two of the most uplifting and unexpected notes.

The first was from my agent, Belinda St. Clair—a sour but persistent old woman who informed me that my short story is at last being considered for publication. To my great delight, a literary journal from a hamlet known as Medicine Hat, Alberta has shown genuine interest in my work. (Who knew that such a thing existed—a review of fiction in the remote provinces of Canada? But Belinda assured me that it is a most reputable independent press with an eye for identifying the rare and overlooked talent.) The fact that my story is under consideration by the esteemed editors of this most obscure and discerning journal causes my heart to race, as if I have been stung by a horsefly.

The second was penned by the delicate hand of my dear Rose and announced that she would arrive in New York on this glorious afternoon. For months now, Rose has been sending me notes—handwritten missives, not those lifeless electronic things—each one filled with the most chilling revelations about her life. I find myself moved by the candor with which she reveals these painful experiences, the incredible honesty, her trust that I shall love her regardless of the indignities that she must endure. My angel! Has there ever, in the history of this great Earth, existed even one woman of such transcendent beauty, such purity of heart, such quiet resolve?

I should note that when I went to bed last night, I checked today's weather report, which was filled with the sourest predictions of thunder, lightning, rain, and severe wind gusts. But after I awoke this morning and prepared my outfit for the day (galoshes, an oilskin jacket and a water-repellant hat), I peered out the window and saw that there was nothing of the sort. I saw only the most perfect cobalt sky above me. And it was only when I opened my front door and found Rose's postcard on my doorstep, only when I learned of her imminent visit, that I understood the cause of this dramatic change in weather: the gods, in honor of this divine guest, decided that they could not defile this day with their putrid micturations.

I check my pocket watch, which indicates that I have just under one hour to reach the Port Authority, the bus terminal where I shall finally, after so many months of our epistolary relationship, meet my dear Rose for the first time. Under normal circumstances, I hold this terminal in the lowest possible regard, and I do so because I am, among many things, an urban planner at heart, and as such I believe that the moment a person enters a city and the moment a person leaves a city should be nothing short of magical. One need only think of the Gare du Nord in Paris or St Pancras in London for proof of the architect's power to exalt, for to walk into such a place is to be inspired with possibility, to marvel at man's great march forward.

But one need only look to the wretched Port Authority (or Penn Station, for that matter) for evidence of the architect's power to deflate even the most optimistic of men, for is it possible to design a building more devoid of beauty, light and human aspiration? Of course it is not possible, as the Port Authority is a building of such soul-sucking power that as soon as one is deposited into its tarry bowels, all hope for a better life is lost and one's descent into the eternal abyss is hastened. But as I walk along the boulevard, I imagine the terminal's appearance in one hour: it shall look not like the dingy hovel that it is, but, transformed by Rose's presence, it shall glisten and sing like Helsinki Central, like Kazansky Station, like the Berlin Hauptbahnhof.

With some trepidation, I traverse the intersection of Broadway, Amsterdam Avenue and 72nd Street—and what a hodgepodge of vectors it is, with cars and trucks, buses and bicycles moving in every which direction and speed. One must be exceedingly careful at this intersection, for I have often seen the inattentive dreamer, his head in the clouds, clipped by a careless taxi. But today my feet are on the ground, and I possess a focus so laser-like that it is as if I am surrounded by an impenetrable force field that guides me unmolested through the chaos and toward my union with Rose.

I stand now in front of a shop that sells both hot dogs and papaya juice, a peculiar combination of savory and sweet that has achieved almost iconic status in New York City. Although I have never stepped inside this shop, I often stand in front and gaze at the people who line up like pups feeding on their mother's teats, and I wonder what it is about these hot dogs and these cups of juice that so captures the imagination of the masses. I once had a professor who opined that "it is a writer's job, no matter how distasteful, to learn about the world"—and as I gaze upon these sodium-rich tubes of meat, with their vulgar mountains of relish, mustard, and sauerkraut, I resolve to sample this fare (but only, of course, in furtherance of my craft).

I look around to confirm that no one I know is nearby and then dash to the end of the line. I put on my dark sunglasses and pull my cap down low over my brow so that I am in a disguised state. Standing in the line before me is a young mother and her little daughter, a delightful girl about seven or eight years old. She is a sprightly lass in a floral sundress and white patent leather sandals, her face beaming with innocence and excitement. And it is this image of a sprightly young girl that causes me to imagine Rose at this same age. I wonder if my dear Rose, too, was once filled with such boundless enthusiasm, dancing on her tippy-toes in anticipation of something so simple as a hot dog and a cup of papaya juice. Yes, yes, I think she was, and I imagine her at this same age dressed too in a floral sundress and white patent leather sandals.

And then my thoughts turn to the rapid arc of a life, how a person can go from this (I look at the sprightly girl) to that (I imagine poor Rose dressed in funereal shades of grey and black, suffering yet another wretched defeat). How, I wonder, can a burgeoning bud turn into a withered flower in the span of just one short season? How does it unfold with such merciless speed? How can a human being's degradation be envisioned and mapped, executed and sealed before that very person has even realized that an irreversible decline has occurred, that a life has been lost?

I smile at the young girl, and when I do so a look crosses her face that suggests a deep fear of me, a revulsion so primal that she might have been looking into the eyes of Grendel himself. I recognize immediately that my familiarity has caused her some distress, so I gaze to the ceiling and assume a rather serious and important pose, a ponderous pose, as if I am giving consideration to matters of the gravest consequence. But it is too late, for the girl slides behind her mother's hip and points at me with a suspicion normally reserved for the vilest of degenerates. The mother follows the girl's finger, follows it right to my face, and passes an immediate judgment upon me (I can tell from her furrowed brow), which causes her to clutch her precious daughter close to her hip.

A feeling of great regret overwhelms me, and I curse my innocence. *Has it come to this?* I wonder. Is it conceivable that we live in a world where a simple smile in a young girl's direction can trigger a cascade of the greatest and most undeserved suspicion? My cheeks are ablaze with humiliation, and I continue to maintain my serious and ponderous pose. I try not to look at the mother and the girl, and I shuffle forward with the line, tethered to it by some invisible band. But then the mother tosses me one more critical look, and it is now too much for me to bear, too much criticism for me to endure. I can think of no logical reaction but to jerk my hand up to my eyes and stare at my pocket watch, conjuring a look of shock that declares my lateness for an important meeting—and, after squinting to suggest that I have confirmed my tardiness, I dart out of the shop.

On the street, I pant and feel as though I have just completed a long swim or an alpine hike, so exhausted am I by this incident with the little girl and her mother and my foolish innocence. To reclaim my breath, I lean over at the waist and rest my palms on my upper legs, and as I do so my cap falls from my head and lands on the ground. I gasp, as this is no ordinary cap, but rather a gift from my late father, Kingsley Walser—war hero, physicist, minor league baseball player, distinguished professor and writer who was short-listed for several prestigious awards.

I can picture him now, walking the canals of New Hope with his walking staff and his old tweed jacket and this very cap, hunched forward, musing about a time when mules pulled barges and men—women, too— worked with their hands. "Bobby," he would say to me, "whatever you do when you grow up, make sure you don't spend too much time living in your head." As I reach for the cap, I smile with tremendous satisfaction, for how proud he would be that I have fulfilled his dream for me!

My fingers are mere centimeters from my beloved cap when the unthinkable occurs: a foot ensconced in a shiny black loafer steps on the cap's brim. I gasp. I wonder if I should grab the cap and pull it out from under the loafer or if I should grab the foot and pull it off the cap. Each option, of course, presents its own set of risks. If I grab the cap, I run the risk of damaging it with the friction that would be generated by both the asphalt and the loafer's sole. If I grab and then lift the trespassing foot, I may very well contribute to some unpleasant interpersonal conflict.

As I in general seek to avoid interpersonal conflict and as I fear damaging my cap, I instead wait for the man to lift his foot. Still bent over at the waist, I hold my hand above the brim, waiting for that moment of opportunity when my cap is emancipated. A few seconds pass—an interminable stretch of time—and the man continues to speak with his female companion, oblivious to the disruption he is causing. At last, the woman comprehends what is going on beneath her and says: "Ivan, I believe you are stepping on this man's *hat*." And when she alerts him to his offensive behavior, he covers his mouth in the most histrionic way and, like a street cur, lifts his leg as if he is planning to urinate on a fire hydrant—at which moment I reach down and snatch the cap.

As I rise to my feet, slapping the cap back into its natural form on my way, I look into the face of the man—and I am stricken with something approximating an uppercut to the solar plexus, for standing before me is none other than Ivan Polsky, chairman emeritus of the English department at Columbia College, effete snob, and editor of a pretentious journal that has on more than one occasion rejected my work with only the rudest and most cursory of notes. "Sorry, not for us," one read. "Sorry, pass," another read in its entirety.

Polsky, my father's former colleague and vanquished adversary, recognizes me and extends his delicate hand.

"Sorry, Bobby, I didn't see your hat... or you for that matter," he lies. I wonder if he must use the word *sorry* in every written and spoken sentence.

"Not a problem, Ivan," I reply and grandly place the cap atop my head as a symbol of my father's superiority over him. Surely he recognizes the meaning of this gesture, and I believe I see him quiver in defeat upon the sight of this cap on my head.

"It is a pleasure to see you, Ivan. Assuming things are well with you?" I ask without even the slightest interest in his well-being. To be polite, I nod to the woman (she blinks furiously) and await an introduction, which does not appear to be forthcoming.

"More than well, Bobby," Polsky parries with the same smugness that once incensed my father. "Much more than well." Without any apparent interest either in *my* well-being or in honoring the most basic rules of social intercourse, Polsky then turns to his female companion and, instead of introducing us, says to her, "Ready to run, hon?" The woman blinks affirmatively, at which point Polsky turns to me.

"Under more ideal circumstances," he says in his insufferable way, "I would go through the formality of introduction, but Annabelle and I really must run. So sorry."

Sorry! he says again. Is he not ashamed of his rote utterances? Apparently not, and in a perverse way I am pleased that he has punctuated our conversation in a manner that validates my low expectation of him, as I have long suspected that a mind so pompous can only operate in the most unimaginative and repetitive ways. I glance at Annabelle, who again blinks, and I wonder if she has a speck of dust in her eye or maybe even some ophthalmic malady—and in a flash, Polsky is gone, his loafers dancing over the pavement like slick porpoises arcing over the great blue sea.

I straighten my spine, lift my shoulders, and continue eastward toward Columbus Avenue, where I shall make a right turn and then walk south toward the Port Authority. I imagine the rapturous embrace that I shall share with Rose when she steps off the bus from Philadelphia, and my pace quickens accordingly. I love this stretch of 72nd Street, for it is one of the few clusters of individual entrepreneurship remaining in this increasingly sterile and corporate city. We have on this street a writer's warmest sanctuary, an old Irish bar that is glorious in its mustiness, its dissipated clientele, and the most delicious shepherd's pie, and there's a family-owned purveyor of mattresses that has been in the neighborhood for almost a century and that sells a pillow-top king that can lull even the most hopeless insomniac into a sublime, Morphean sleep.

But all is not well on this street, for, like a mole poking its head out of a hole in the most beautifully manicured croquet green, a craven intruder has appeared. Here, on the south side of the street, a noxious chain store—a competitor of the family-owned mattress shop—has recently devoured and metabolized an old pharmacy, ingesting in the process (I imagine) a cornucopia of amphetamines and tranquilizers, erectile medication, eye patches, adult diapers, and bunion scrapers. The store—sick and high from its gluttony, an arriviste of the lowest form—leers across the street at its modest, tasteful rival and flaunts its newfound wealth.

I peer into this store, with its shameless salesmen and its predatory financing plans (and not a divine pillow-top to be seen). With my lips curled and my nose pinched, I make a threatening, judgmental face, hoping that the salesman leaning against the front door can detect my loathing. But as is so common with this particular type of man, he mistakes my disgust for the keenest interest in his second-rate wares, and before I can dash away unaccosted, he is out of the store and on my elbow like a yellow jacket on a slice of peach cobbler.

"How may I help you?" I ask with indignation.

The man, short and powerful with the outsized shoulders of a Greco-Roman wrestler, takes a step back and offers a look of such unjustifiable confidence that I gasp at his temerity.

"I saw you look in the store and figure you probably need a new bed," he says. "And we're the best game in town."

"The best game in town?" I chuckle. "What makes you think this is some sort of game?" The man appears confused. (No surprise.) "Yes," I continue, "this is no game. Far from it." I nod in the direction of the store across the street. "Tell me, do you and your fellow mountebanks take some twisted pleasure in trying to drive those decent people out of business? All the while offering goods of an inferior quality? Is that how you operate?"

The salesman grunts. "Just business," he says with a disdain that further infuriates me.

"Just business? Mere seconds ago you described this little competition as a game, but now it has miraculously transformed into *business*?"

The man stares at me for a few seconds, the muscles in his jaw twitching as if he is experiencing a mild seizure.

"Why don't you come inside," he offers, "and you can try out the platinum line. We got great terms, and we're even running a sale today—just for today."

"A sale!" I burst out in laughter. "How convenient. On the very day that you are trying to sell me an inferior and overpriced bed, on the very day that I am least likely to purchase a new bed, you just happen to be running a sale. I think not!"

The salesman sighs in defeat and looks at his watch, a garish steel and gold thing that hangs loosely around his wrist—and I believe that I am winning this lopsided war of attrition.

"Fine," he says, "whatever." Then he bows in a condescending manner and retreats to his fluorescent showroom, a vile den that emits a gaseous aura of death.

Replete with the satisfaction of a rival defeated, I continue my journey eastward, doffing my cap in the direction of the old bed store across the street.

"Hats off," I call out, denouncing globalization in my subtle yet powerful way, one that is discernible only to the most observant sociologist.

I have long maintained that the most effective means of breaking the gelid grip of uniformity is to purchase goods and services not from the smarmy salesmen that proliferate as if produced in some dystopian laboratory, but rather from the eccentric, the genuine, the infrequent. One has a choice to participate in this free market, I have maintained, and to direct one's dollars either to the homogeneous or to the peculiar; and after many years of refusing to buy what we are directed to buy, often suffering great additional expense and inconvenience in the process, slowly crushing these powerful forces, one shall be relieved to see the muscular bed salesman close up shop and seek other employment. About this very issue, my father once said something profound—something, I recall, having to do with a checkbook, a vote, and considerable patience.

A young woman with an elegant gait and a confident air now approaches from Columbus Avenue, and I am delighted to be distracted from my heavy theories on the marketplace and personal empowerment. The woman speaks into her phone, so immersed is she in her conversation that she appears unaware of her surroundings, and walks with so much authority against the flow of pedestrian traffic that streams of people are redirected from her path.

As she sashays past me, exuding the most vital, feminine energy, my thoughts of course turn to Rose. Dear Rose. If only my sweet dove could muster just one-tenth the confidence of this woman, I think, then she could achieve all of the potential that her great but unrealized talents justify. But Rose sadly possesses no such confidence, so crushed is she by the troubles of life, so dispirited by wicked forces beyond her control.

After I turn the corner on Columbus and make my way south toward the bus terminal, I spy a corner store, in front of which is a spectacular botanical display. I stand before the wall of flowers and consider what might most delight Rose. On the top shelf, farthest away from a thief's reach, are several buckets of roses: red, white, yellow, pink—even a pale blue. (Does such a thing, a blue rose, exist in nature, or is this merely the creation of some crazed botanist?) All lovely and regal, they are, but to purchase roses for Rose would be too obvious a pun and would relegate me to the trash heap of the banal. Next to the roses is a bucket of carnations, a tacky flower that infuriates me with its affectations. My deceased mother, an avid gardener, maintained a strict no-carnations policy in our home, going so far as to advise guests that any such flowers brought as gifts would, despite the giver's generosity, be summarily discarded.

Beside the carnations is a cluster of tulips—pastel yellow, pink and orange—the flower of birth, of *re*-birth. And what more appropriate flower could there be for my dear Rose? For does the tulip not signify everything that I hope for her and everything that she must surely hope for herself? To be light and colorful, to hibernate in a brick of frozen sod, to spring forth from the damp, vernal earth, to bask and sway in the sun's regenerating rays, to capture the attention of every admiring passerby?

I note the price on a placard and hand a ten-dollar bill to the attendant, a tiny Andean man with a flat nose and a bewildered smile that suggests some confusion as to how he has come to live in this world. (I, too, have experienced this same confusion.) I check my watch and see that I have approximately thirty-eight minutes until Rose's arrival. As such, I quicken my pace down Columbus past its intersection with Broadway and then arrive at Lincoln Center, a vision of such stunning design that my heart races with excitement. I inhale the great Chagall tapestries—so rich in hue and motion—the textured crème travertine façades, the playful fountain in the plaza's center. I am uplifted, exalted by the grandeur of the vision—and can think of the Port Authority and its benighted architect only with rage.

My journey south takes me through some vague, ill-defined point at which Columbus mutates into Ninth Avenue and vice versa. I chuckle at man's pretensions, the belief that a change in name—a rechristening—can invest a street with elegance and desirability: Sixth Avenue transformed into Avenue of the Americas, Fourth Avenue into Park, Tenth into Amsterdam, Eleventh into West End.

Tulips in hand, I cross 57th Street and enter a neighborhood called Hell's Kitchen. I once met a man who grew up here, a friend of my father's from the Army. I encountered him once or twice when I was a child and recall being impressed with the size of his hands—huge, animal-like paws—and a thick scar that ran across his throat from ear to ear, the result of having been garroted not far from where I now stand. But the Hell's Kitchen of the past, with its Irish and Germans and its vicious gangs, is a distant memory, for the neighborhood is now saturated with expensive apartments and pricey restaurants and bars from which hang rainbow flags. Yes, rainbow flags of all sizes adorn most every bar and restaurant in Hell's Kitchen. How festive it is here!

A man stands in front of one of these rainbow bars. He is a fit man in a tight, sleeveless shirt, and he smiles and waves to me as if I am an old friend whom he has not seen in years. He waves to me with a kindness that earlier escaped the vapid Stavros, and I am inspired to wave back with a comparable smile.

"How ya doing?" he says with the easy cadence of the Southern gentleman.

"How ya doing?" I reply, careful to mimic his casual banter so that he does not think me stiff and joyless.

"No worries," he calls. The man speaks with a cheerfulness that even a misanthrope would find intoxicating.

I gaze at the rainbow flag, which snaps like crisp linen against the cerulean sky. "No worries," I counter with identical cheer, doffing my hat—a kick in my step as I stride onward to the Port Authority, which is visible now in the distance.

I imagine Rose's bus maneuvering at this moment over the city's surface streets, my precious dove gazing out at the city's hubbub, her sweet breath fogging the window, her heart beating in anticipation of our imminent union. My heart, too, beats in anticipation; my palms are moist, and the fine hairs on my forearms tickle and dance. I check my pocket watch and see that in only several minutes, Rose and I shall at last be united—and

I imagine that we shall hug each other with an ardor reserved for the returning soldier and his joyful wife.

I cross 42nd Street (here, alas, stands yet another hot dog and papaya stand) and make my way to the bus terminal. After pausing to observe the building's bland exterior, I step into this sarcophagus and, just as I had imagined, this dark and wretched place has been transformed by Rose's visit into a glistening palace fit for a tsarina.

The ceilings of the terminal, so low that under normal circumstances they would compress a man's very spine, have now risen like an astral vault, a firmament that inspires even the most diffident to glide through this hard life with resoluteness. The floors, once an endless, dull slab, radiate now like the finest granite, while shafts of ambient light penetrate the thick, windowless walls and bathe the interior in a warm glow.

I stand in front of a sign and search for the gate from which my dear Rose, like a debutante at a cotillion, shall emerge. The sign assures me that the Philadelphia bus will be arriving at the gate in less than two minutes. My heart thumping, I glide up the escalator, increasing the machine's speed with my own two-step leaps, and quickly reach the second floor. There, I turn to the right, run a few more feet and gasp when I see the gate before me—and arriving at the very same moment, the manifestation of some perfect synchronicity, is the bus from Philadelphia! I stand several feet from the gate's door, my posture straight and tall, the bouquet of tulips held before me.

The doors of this bus—of this chariot—open with a sensuous, pneumatic hiss, and I await Rose's exit. I wonder where in the bus she is seated—fore or aft—and conclude that, given her lack of esteem, she is unlikely to be seated in the front. Poor Rose, relegating herself without justification to the back of the bus. Why must she be so cruel to herself? Is not the world already too cruel to her? Why must she aid and abet this heinous crime?

The first person out of the bus is an elderly woman who moves at a pace so glacial that I fear hours may pass before the next passenger is liberated. This woman holds on to the bus railing with such a tight grip, like a mechanized claw, that it is hard to imagine how blood can flow through the veins of her corrugated hand. The woman makes little progress, and I curse this delay. Have Rose and I not waited long enough for this union? Have we not suffered more than any inchoate lovers must suffer? The old woman shifts her foot a few inches on the stair, disinclined to take a full step downward. My heart races at the sight of this malicious crone. I glare at her and see in her face a certain coldness, one that must surely have caused an estrangement from her children.

The woman eyes the pavement below and takes one delicate step downward. Again, she freezes, and it is as if the Earth has stopped its rotation. I imagine Rose penned in behind a line of passengers, her heart pounding, and I consider grabbing this spiteful hag by the arm and pulling her off the bus myself. But just then, the woman releases the rail and skips off the bus as if she were a gymnast! What has caused this transformation I do not know, but when she passes me, she smiles and says, "Good day, sweetheart."

My frozen heart thaws in an instant. "Good day," I reply to this lovely octogenarian.

Several passengers depart the bus without incident, and I feel the energy of Rose's soul comingle with mine. She is so close that we are now communicating at a molecular level, our masses intertwining. I glance up at the row of shaded windows on the side of the bus, through which I can see not faces but the silhouettes of the few remaining passengers. There, at the very end, is a woman of modest build, just like my Rose. I look down to the tulips and notice that one petal has fallen limp. I remove it with great care and place it in my pocket, turning the bouquet around so that its flaw is not apparent.

I again look up at the female figure, the one at the end of the line, and I count the seconds until she reaches the front of the bus. She moves quickly and presents her bare lower leg in the aperture of the door, hesitates in order to tantalize me and steps out of the bus. Oh, how beautiful she is, how elegant and understated, not like those vulgar women who compensate for their deficiencies by bringing attention to their strengths. She approaches me and I smile, extending the tulips in her direction. She too smiles, and it is at this precise moment that our souls liquefy, mix and fuse.

I glance down at the flowers, then back to her, awaiting her reach. But rather than accept this gift, she walks right past me. How mischievous of her, how playful! I shall go along with her clever game. I shall wait for her to stop and pivot, then run into my arms. And we shall both have a great laugh over this, a fine start to a lifetime of gaiety. Rose keeps walking, though much farther than I would have expected for a joke of this nature. Our comedic timing appears to be slightly misaligned, but that is a problem easily fixed through familiarity.

There is a middle-aged woman, nicely dressed, who waits near the far wall. She scans the departing passengers, and when she sees Rose, she waves her hands like a madwoman, screams, and runs to her, giving my love an exuberant hug and a kiss on the cheek. I wonder who this woman is and why she, too, is here to greet Rose. As I take a step in their direction, flowers in hand, Rose and this woman cross arms, lean close together, and skip toward the escalator, talking as they go.

I freeze as I realize that this woman is not my Rose, that I have been mistaken. Deflated, I turn back to the bus just in time for the driver to close the doors, the pneumatic hiss signaling an empty coach. I walk over to the bus and knock on the glass panel of the door. As if I have just asked him to donate an organ, the driver sighs and then opens the doors.

"I'm sorry, sir, but is there anyone left in the bus?" I ask, sure that Rose must have fallen asleep in the back, so deeply in fact that she does not know the bus has arrived, that her beloved awaits.

"Just me," the driver replies.

"You sure?"

"I'm sure," he says somewhat gruffly, then closes the doors, again with that intolerable hiss.

I stand in a state of disbelief, as this is the third time that Rose, despite her assurances, has failed to step off the bus from Philadelphia. Each time, I have received a letter shortly thereafter expressing great remorse and explaining in only the vaguest terms the crises and assaults that have prevented her from boarding the bus. And how honorable of her, the poor girl, to spare me the horrible details of her degradation, for I could barely contain my anguish if I knew one bit more. I pray of course that Rose is safe, that whatever has kept her from me this time can be endured without greater damage to her fragile psyche, for the poor girl has, like Joan of Arc, suffered more than any woman should suffer.

I walk toward the escalator and look around the terminal, which too feels the pain of my disappointment, for how it has transformed over just the past few minutes. The ceilings have dropped to their original claustrophobia-inducing height, and the walls now refuse all light, as if they are draped in curtains of lead. And about the terminal walk not human beings, but some mutated species that cannot comprehend the gravity of its own despair. I drop my shoulders, for in Rose's absence the terminal has reverted to form.

Out on the street, I wonder how I shall return home. I am tired from my long walk, and returning on foot is unappealing. There is the subway or the public bus, but I am at present in no mood to join the masses, as lovely and earnest as they may be. I look to the far corner of 42nd Street and there stands a regal steed attached by silver ropes to a carriage. The cab is pristine, lacquered white with a white canvas top and driven by a man in a tailored suit and black top hat, a monocle over his right eye, muttonchops framing his angular face. The man appears to have been transported from a distant era.

I approach the carriage.

"Driver," I say, "would you be so kind as to take me to 72nd Street and West End Avenue?"

The driver nods and shakes the reins, prompting me to step up into the cab. I take a seat on the leather banquette and admire the carriage's fine mahogany trim, polished and rich. I look to the sky and notice that an inky cloud, thick in the core, with menacing tentacles, slides to the west and blocks the light of the sun, throbbing like some awful sea creature. A brisk wind now whips in from the river, cold and damp, and a chill overtakes me. I reach for the tartan blanket beside me and drape it over my lap.

With another snap of the reins, we begin our journey home. I glance at the driver, at his profile, and I see on his monocled, mutton-chopped face a look of regret, one that conveys the horror of his anachronism. Like so many, he has been expelled from his proper place; he lives in the wrong place at the wrong time, and he must at all times carry with him the pain of his dislocation. I, too, have experienced such a dislocation, and my heart thus aches for this man. I lean forward and offer the tulips to the driver, who eyes them first with suspicion, then, after a shrug of the shoulders, accepts them with a grateful nod. He places them on the seat to his right and shakes the reins, and I am soothed by the possibility that I have relieved the suffering of another human being.

The sound of hooves on pavement—*clippity-clop, clippity-clop*—is at first calming, metronomic, but then something about this cadence triggers in me a recollection, a hazy recollection that I cannot fully recall, a mere shard of a memory that—*clippity-clop, clippity-clop*—emanates from some dark and distant place. I experience a pinch in my stomach and turn to the side, my shoulder pressed hard against the edge of the carriage.

I reach for this memory, but it remains elusive. My mind, in pursuit, lunges and grasps, as if trying to catch a clever fly. Several times, I come within a filament's width of capturing this memory, only to lose it in the darkness of the mind. After a few moments of frustration, however, the pinch in my stomach releases and a recollection bursts forth in a flash.

I close my eyes and see myself as a young child. My father, just returned from a trip to Holland, sports on his feet colorful clogs and presents a small pair for me. I slip my tiny feet into the wooden shoes—they fit perfectly!—and my father shows me a *klompen* dance. Leg up and leg down, heel to toe. Leg up and leg down, heel to toe. *Clippity-clop, clippity-clop.* I follow his lead, delighted by this war hero, this physicist, this minor league baseball player, this distinguished professor and writer—this klompen dancer.

The carriage moves northward, and I wonder why it is that our most joyous memories, rather than offering comfort, often invoke in us the greatest pain. As the ache of this recollection is too uncomfortable for me to bear, I quickly purge the image of my late father's klompen dance and, to distract myself, focus instead on the construction and design of this great carriage. Above me is a canopy made of thick white canvas reminiscent of a schooner's sail; on either side of the vehicle are sconces that, I imagine, would cast the warmest glow during an evening ride; the interior doors are covered in a regal purple velvet; and beneath me, between the two wheels, is a metal step positioned perfectly between seat and pavement. Tethered to the side of the carriage is a wooden bucket, a feed bucket, which claps against the door and announces every pothole and divot. And it is this bucket that evokes in me yet another distant memory.

With unspeakable grief, I picture the tortured face of my dear mother at the moment of her death—and then the empty wash bucket near her fallen body. I recall her affection for me, how she defended me (and my peculiarities) with the abandon of a cornered tigress.

"Don't worry, sweetheart," she would tell me, "there's no shame in having your head in the clouds." And when I once cried to her about my fear of being alone, about my fear of never finding a girl who would delight in what I must concede is a certain eccentricity on my part, she rubbed my hand and said to me, "Robert, you *will* find someone...and if not, you'll always have me."

The stallion before me slows, and as I wonder if this noble beast understands my grief, I experience the slightest constriction of the throat, a fleeting apnea and a gasp for air. I brace myself against the cold wind, struggling to draw a breath into my lungs. As the carriage moves west, I glance over to the fading bus terminal. "Rose," I mutter with the deepest sorrow. "Dear Rose." I turn my face to the harsh wind and lift the blanket up over my shoulders, the brim of my cap pulled down low so that I can neither see nor be seen.

Two

A fortnight has now passed since my dearest Rose was forced by what must have been the most unexpected circumstances to abort her journey to New York, and since our failed rendezvous I have suffered from a debilitating sickness that has manifested in a swelling of the neck's lymph nodes, a low-grade fever, and an achiness in the joints of the upper extremities. Given my acute infirmity, I have remained housebound, unable to gather even the modest strength necessary to tend to my most basic daily tasks.

There is a young man—a Doctor Seamus Kilkenny of Columbia Presbyterian—who often enjoys the vanilla crullers served by Stavros. He is a renowned physician, and when the peculiar restaurateur informed him of my illness, the doctor was kind enough to call upon me at my home yesterday. After the most confident knock on the door (oh how cocksure these doctors are!), he entered my chamber and introduced himself with a formality that was

unbefitting two men who have exchanged frequent pleas-
antries before the pastry case. I felt obliged to mention to
him the irony of a Kilkenny being employed by a Presbyterian institution, and when I did so the man seemed
unamused—irritated, even—and I thus resolved to limit
our interaction only to the professional matters of diagnosis, treatment, and prognosis.

This Kilkenny quickly went about his business. He
probed and prodded me, palpating my neck and cheeks,
taking my temperature, and placing the chilly head of the
stethoscope to my chest and back. After concluding his
inspection of my body with a befuddled shake of the head,
the eager physician turned his attention to my surroundings, examining my chamber and possessions with all
the keenness of Sherlock Holmes. I thought him impertinent as he opened the cupboard and read the labels of
my cleaning solutions and plant fertilizers, as he surveyed
my refrigerator and peered into the drain of my sink—and
when I asked him to state his intentions, he informed me
that he was searching for, perhaps, some environmental
cause of my illness.

"Is there not a *biological* cause?" I asked, somewhat
affronted.

Kilkenny waved his hand in front of his nose as if
he had detected a foul odor. "I can point to nothing that
would indicate a microbial illness, which leads me to believe that you may be suffering from an environmental
toxin. An allergy. Or, possibly..." The doctor assumed an
arrogant posture that reminded me of none other than the
supercilious Polsky. "... or possibly a psycho-emotional
trauma of some sort."

"A psycho-emotional trauma?" I snapped, outraged

at the suggestion that anything but a virulent virus or bacterium could be the cause of my illness. I considered denouncing the doctor for the impostor he had revealed himself to be—but instead smiled, tucked in my shirt, and led him to the door with the elegance of the seasoned usher guiding a patron to his box at the opera. Thereupon, I thanked Kilkenny for both his earnest commitment to the oath of Hippocrates and the kindness extended to me, then pulled a five-dollar bill from my wallet and handed it to him. A look of surprise crossed the man's face, and I can only imagine that he was shocked by my generosity.

After the quack departed, I retreated to my bed and fell into the deepest of sleeps, awakening this morning in a state of remarkable and unexpected health. My recovery was nothing short of miraculous. My temperature has returned to normalcy; my lumpy, swollen neck is once again taut and thin; and the aches and pains that made even the most minor movement agonizing have receded like the tide. I stand now before the bathroom mirror and observe my face, the skin so fresh, my hazel eyes clear and glistening. A great miracle—I appear to have been fully restored to my healthy state, and the timing could not be more perfect, for today I have been called upon to uphold a citizen's most important civic responsibility: jury duty.

My father once told me that for such a serious, jurisprudential ritual a citizen must dress in a manner that demonstrates the proper respect for not only the esteemed courts, the judges, and the law itself, but for the defendant and for one's peers as well. So I pull from the closet my finest suit—a navy blue gabardine with the thinnest of chalk stripes—a starched white dress shirt, a grey silk cravat, and an ostrich belt bequeathed to me by my father. I dress and stand before the mirror. I turn from side to side and admire the cut of the suit, perfect except for a slight buckle under the arms. The silk cravat glistens against the starched linen shirt, and my father's cuff links peek out from slivers in my shirt's French cuffs. I glance down to my black loafers that announce, I imagine, both my law-abiding nature and a certain nimbleness of body and spirit. I am pleased by my impressive visage, one that conveys the highest character, and I hope that the barristers too will be so impressed and that they will entrust me to decide the fate of another human being.

As I am about to place the cap atop my head, I take one more look in the mirror—side to side—and find that I am no longer pleased with my attire. I fear that I may lack a certain flair, one that would guarantee my admission into the exclusive fraternity of jurors. So I pull from my dresser drawer a blue kerchief with tiny white roses. I smile, for how my dear Rose continues to show herself to me in the most subtle and unexpected ways. I fold the kerchief and place it in my lapel pocket, tugging at its folds, fluffing it up so that it conveys a creativity of thought and not the prickliness and dogmatism that may offend the barristers. Now fully satisfied, I exit my apartment.

My destination is the Church Street courthouse downtown. I look around and see that the traffic appears to be in a state of the most extreme congestion. I thus make my way down 72nd Street toward the subway, a method of transportation that I have used only twice in my life: once when my father took me to the Bronx for a baseball game between the New York Yankees and a team from Detroit—and then a second time, by mistake, when in that dreadful Penn Station I intended to board an Amtrak train destined for Boston but instead stepped onto something called an R train that took me all the way to the borough of Queens. I pass Stavros's restaurant (it is closed) and pause to eye the many delights inside the pastry case. Furious that here stands in vain an eager patron who desires to purchase a chocolate bear claw, I resolve to have a discussion with Stavros regarding the basic principles of commerce.

I continue to Broadway and with great dread enter the subway, where I purchase a ticket from an automated kiosk. When I do so, I recall with some nostalgia the day on which my father handed me a subway token and I dropped it into the slot, awaited the click, and pushed my way through the turnstile—then downward to an unknown subterranean world with the eager anticipation of a spelunker descending into the mysterious darkness.

I now stand on the platform and peer down to the filthy tracks below. Refuse of all kinds is strewn about, and I wonder what kind of human being would throw a water bottle or a diaper or a prophylactic to the tracks. An animal scurries about in the trash—whether a rodent or a terrier, I do not know—and I am revolted by the scene before me. In the distance, I see the flickering light of the oncoming train. I look around at the crowd, members of which jockey for position, and I fear that I may be pushed—inadvertently or not—off the platform and down to the tracks below. I eye the lethal third rail and recall a news article I read years ago about a suicidal man who lay down on the tracks and grabbed the electrified metal; already dead from the voltage, the man was then run over by a train, and while his body was pulled several hundred feet down the tracks, his severed hand remained clasped to the rail. I picture that bloody hand, a grip of death around the metal, and wonder about the things we hold on to that are harmful to us, fatal even—and how we refuse to let go even when all hope is lost.

I step back several feet, a safe distance from the edge of the platform, and await the train's arrival. Soon the doors lurch open, and I am pleased to see that numerous seats are free. I take one and look at the faces around me—white, black, Asian, Hispanic, indeterminable, and variations thereof—and wonder if any of these good souls might too be on their way to the sacred proceeding of *voir dire*. I wonder if I might serve on a jury with one of my fellow travelers, arguing with them arcane points of law and equity. And might one of these fellow travelers be an irksome holdout—the only juror to refuse to convict or acquit—and might I be forced to prevail upon such an obstructionist with the full force of my intellect?

By the time we reach the Columbus Circle station, the subway car is full, with all of the seats taken and two old men and a pregnant woman standing with discomfort. The pregnant woman is so swollen, so distended, that she is liable to produce a child at any moment, and she leans backward, palms on her lower back, to relieve, I presume, the pressure of this life inside her. My father was a stickler for extending courtesy to the infirm and to the fairer sex—doors opened, umbrellas raised, chairs positioned—and on that ride to Yankee Stadium when I was a young boy, I watched as he stood for an old woman with a cane and then nodded to me—a subtle direction for me to take note, which I most certainly did. As I now look around the car, I notice several needy passengers who would no doubt delight in my generosity and the ability to sit comfortably.

I consider the two aged men who hold on to the same metal pole. They are speaking to each other with the deepest familiarity, engaging in a rather animated conversation, and I conclude that they are the oldest of friends—two men who no doubt grew up together in the same neighborhood. (Was it Washington Heights? Little Italy? Sunnyside?) They have, I imagine, served in the same Army unit, surviving one, maybe two, wars; they have spent every Memorial Day together with their families at Jones Beach; for decades, they have dined once a week at the same Italian restaurant on Mulberry Street, enjoying clams oreganata and fried calamari and a carafe of Montepulciano d'Abruzzo.

I turn my attention to the pregnant woman and watch as she grimaces from the pain in her abdomen. I decide that she is in greater need than the two old friends, and I stand, vacating my seat with a debonair step to the side. There stands nearby a young man, an able-bodied young man, slack-eyed and sloppy, who exudes an indolence that makes me tremble, for I fear that he will take advantage of my kind gesture and lay claim to the seat before the pregnant woman has a chance to react. Our eyes meet, and I toss him a menacing glare that has the intended effect, for he gasps upon recognition of my moral superiority and retreats to the other side of the car.

I stare at the pregnant woman, and she reciprocates, offering the most plaintive, beseeching look. With my left arm I make a grand, sweeping gesture that—as if I am a magician—starts high above my shoulder and ends with my hand, palm up, pointing toward the open seat.

"If you'd like, Madame, *please* take this seat," I say magnanimously.

The woman blushes and nods in appreciation. She smiles. She rubs her belly in a circular, clockwise motion and takes the empty seat. "Thank you," she says with the gratitude of the desert wanderer who is given a canteen of cool, spring water.

I look over to the old men, who break from their conversation and nod in appreciation of my chivalrous act. As we approach the Times Square station, the train shimmies and lunges, causing the men to stumble forward, and only by holding on to the pole are they able to remain upright. The train stops in the station, the doors open, and the men smile at each other in recognition of a harm barely avoided—and I wonder if they have evaded many more serious threats on the battlefield. They look to see if any seats have opened and, disappointed, continue to clutch the pole.

I review the faces of the seated passengers around me. There are three prim elderly women, a chubby man with a crooked cane, and a young mother with a sniffling toddler by her side—all of whom, my father would argue, are entitled to retain their seats because of the challenges they face. At the far end of the row, however, now sits the young man—slack-eyed and sloppy, indolently at ease—who earlier recoiled at my menacing glare. In his hand is a phone, and he appears to be playing a game on the device. He does not once glance up at the two old men who cling to the pole, either because he is so immersed in the game or because he is ashamed of his callous behavior. I suspect it is the former. I grant him a few moments to recognize the error of his ways, and when he does not so much as look away from his tiny, flashing screen, I become consumed with the fury that often results when one witnesses a wrong committed against the disadvantaged or the weak.

The two old men struggle to hold the pole, and I resolve to confront this insensitive young man. I take a few steps to the side, so that I am now standing before him, and clear my throat in a manner designed to attract his attention. But my efforts are for naught, for the man wears headphones that are surely pumping loud sounds into his ears, and he thus cannot hear me. So instead I tap the man's sneaker with the tip of my loafer and await his response. But the young man does not react! He merely moves his sneaker and continues the mad movements of his fingers across the screen. Enraged by his insularity, his refusal to connect with the world around him, I tap him on the shoulder—a bold act that catches his attention. He looks up to me and pulls the wires from his ears.

"Yeah?" he says.

I offer him my most serious expression—lower jaw jutting slightly forward, eyes squinting. "You are a young, able-bodied man, fit and trim, are you not?"

The young man stares at me as if I have said something offensive. "Creep," he mutters.

Only modestly wounded, I ignore his salvo and continue with the task at hand. "There are two old men, right on that pole over there, and I am sure that they would be grateful for the chance to sit. Perhaps you might give your seat to one of them."

The young man eyes the old friends from Washington Heights or Little Italy or Sunnyside. Surely, he must see the struggle with which they attempt to keep their footing. I await a humane response, but instead he shrugs his shoulders, returns the headphones to his ears and taps away at the screen of his phone as if he exists on a planet of one.

I am enraged. I consider my options. One possibility is for me to unleash a harangue on this insolent sloth and shame him into proper action. But I then consider the man's likely response—disregard for both the tone and the substance of my argument—and then dismiss that plan as nothing more than foolish naïveté. I concede that I may very well be dealing with a man incapable of introspection and change. Another possibility is for me to resort to physicality, to intimidate him with some show of force, as I have often seen in the cinema. But I quickly admit that I am not a man capable of such things.

I recall with sadness the day I returned home from school—was it third grade, fourth?—with a bloody lip and a grape-sized welt above my eye. My father inquired with great concern about the cause of my injury, and when I told him that a schoolyard bully had pummeled me, he led me to the driveway and demonstrated to me the proper technique for defending oneself against physical violence and imposing it upon others. I now picture with a shiver the awkward motions I made, as if I were shooing away an irksome fly—and I recall my father's exasperation. I look down at the young man and glare as we approach 34th Street. When the train stops and the door opens, the lazy man stands slowly—as if he has not a care in the world—and exits the train. Aha! I think, my menacing stare has delivered a powerful message. My bark, as they say, is greater than my bite.

I turn to the elderly men and point to the empty seat, which I now block with my body to prevent another interloper.

"Gentleman," I say. "A seat has become unoccupied, and I thought that one of you, given your … your *circumstance*, would prefer to sit."

The two men turn to each other and smile, moved no doubt by my compassion for the plight of the elderly. (Oh how badly they are treated, the elderly! How society devalues these aged souls for no good reason other than their funny smells and their proximity to death.)

The frailer of the two raises his hand to me like the Pope standing before the masses. "We're good standin', thanks. Sittin's no good, ya know." I recall the accent of my father's Army friend, the one with the huge, animal-like paws. Hell's Kitchen, I think. These old men are from Hell's Kitchen— the rough neighborhood that existed *prior* to the rainbow flags.

I fear that I have insulted them. I am surprised by their vibrancy, and I laugh at the folly of the human mind. I consider the process through which even the most well-intentioned brain can create false narratives and manufacture conclusions that appear to be based on the most reliable information, but that instead rely on flawed assumptions. As the lights of the subway car flicker and darken, I wonder how many wars have resulted from this type of misunderstanding, this application of belief to what appears to be an irrefutable fact pattern, only for it to be discovered that these facts were not what they appeared to be. How frustrating is man's inability to see clearly what stands right before him. Yes, yes, how frustrating it is that we seem to be designed—by

God Himself—to misinterpret the very world around us.

I sit down and tip my cap to the gentlemen. As I still suffer minor residual effects from my illness, I am relieved to be seated. The remainder of the ride downtown passes without incident, and the existence of several open seats mercifully relieves me of any sense of obligation to the needy and infirm. After another ten minutes of being transported through this dark and dismal tube, I disembark at my destination and ascend to the street, to the glorious light where I am reunited with the happy, sunbathed masses.

I stand on the corner and look around for the courthouse. In the distance, I see its grand limestone façade and a row of columns that beckon me with their vertical precision. I maneuver through a Bedouin's camp of hotdog carts, peanut vendors, and rug merchants and enter the marmoreal lobby of this edifice, where I am subjected to the great indignity of being forced through an x-ray machine to ensure that I do not possess any weapons. (I do own an antique walking staff in which is hidden a sharp dagger, and I am grateful that I did not bring it to court today.)

My trip through this machine causes quite a stir, as loud bells and sirens catch the attention of not one but three security guards, who quickly surround me. They ask permission to place their hands on my body, and I accede, as who can deny an official request of such a nature? A female guard, a buxom woman—Samoan or Tongan, perhaps—asks me to spread my legs and raise my arms above my head, which I do without protestation. She slides her meaty hands over my arms, my back and chest, my ribs, then down to my legs and—to my great surprise—not my groin, but to the area immediately surrounding my groin. I flinch at the lengths to which she must go to fulfill her duties.

The guard steps back and nods. "Clear," she yells, signaling that I am free to continue.

I follow the signs to the jury room and, when I enter, am met by the sight of dozens of prospective jurors milling about a room the size of a tennis court. It is a curious communion of young and old, prosperous and indigent, races known and unknown. I approach a man, a bailiff, in a crisp white uniform. I hand him my jury summons, an official document personally signed by none other than the Mayor of the great City of New York (a man who offends me with his arrogance and his disregard for the most basic consideration of punctuality). The bailiff, a grim man whom I suspect is irritated by crying babies and tourists, glances at my summons and points to a row of chairs. "There," he commands. "Wait there."

I obey and take my seat. Soon, a clerk—a wiry, ashen man reminiscent of a defeated bureaucrat in one of Gogol's sad stories—calls out a list of names. Upon hearing the Walser surname announced, I leap to my feet and, joining the others, approach the clerk.

"Follow me," he says glumly. "We're going to courtroom number eight, the Honorable Ambrose Felice presiding."

I look around and assess the other prospective jurors, attempting to determine if they are more or less likely than I to be chosen. I make several superficial observations about these people (this one looks supremely dimwitted, that one has a tuft of hair growing out of her pointed chin, another wears a stained shirt) and in doing so I buttress my own sense of standing—but then the dim-witted one smiles kindly at me and I curse myself for my pretensions and my arrogance. I recall the painful taunts to which I myself was subjected in the schoolyard, the bullies' ridicule of my thin build, my wire-rimmed glasses, my peculiar nature—and I now wonder who I am to judge another human being based solely on their appearance? And is it not true that one's appearance has nothing to do with the substance of a person, their ability to serve as a juror with dispassion and objectivity? And, further, could it even be that idiosyncrasy of appearance might actually indicate the most sober judicial temperament? For is that person not less prone to the persuasion of the superficial?

We are seated in rows facing the judge's lofty perch. The Honorable Ambrose Felice is a corpulent man with a sprawling, gin-blossomed nose and the wild silver hair of a Bohemian.

"Welcome, ladies and gentlemen, and thank you for fulfilling your civic duty to our judicial system. Today we are choosing jurors for case number 07006-19, *People of the State of New York v. Stavros.*" I gasp when I hear this name—*Stavros*—and wonder if this defendant could be related to the strange restaurateur. Or whether it could be Stavros himself!

Impossible, I think. The Greek's oddness in business judgment and his impenetrable aloofness aside, I have always known him to be even in temperament and upstanding in matters relating to ethics. (Once, when a confused Hungarian tourist mistakenly gave him twenty dollars instead of five and then exited the diner, Stavros ran down the street after her—galloped, really—waving the twenty and yelling until he caught her attention and corrected the error.)

"The facts of this case are as follows," the judge continues. "The defendant operates a restaurant establishment on West 72nd Street in Manhattan." I gasp so loudly that the judge stops and looks at me.

"Is there something wrong, sir?" he says to me with an authority that makes me tremble and sweat.

"No, your Honor, no. My apologies." My hands shake, my forehead is now covered in a film of perspiration, and I fear that my shirt will soon be drenched.

The judge eyes the bailiff and then me, and I wonder if I shall be expelled for my indecorous outburst.

"The defendant operates a restaurant, and it is alleged that two witnesses, two women who intended to marry— to marry *each other*—came into this establishment and asked the defendant, Mr. Stavros, to make a cake for their wedding. It is further alleged that Mr. Stavros refused to make this wedding cake on the grounds that he does not believe in marriage between members of the same sex and that his religious beliefs permit him to deny goods and services to the complainants. It is also alleged that Mr. Stavros communicated this position to the two women and, after a heated argument among the parties, expelled the complainants from his restaurant." The judge runs a hand through his thick mane. "The defendant has been charged with a violation of Article 6, Section 3 of the New York State Criminal Code, which prohibits discrimination by businesses against people based upon race, religion, creed, gender, age, and, as of the first of this year, sexual orientation or sexual identity."

I picture the vague look on Stavros's face and consider

the incomprehensible idiocy that compels a man to close a restaurant during the busiest hours. I wonder if it is possible that the Greek would deny two women—two women in love—the pleasure of eating one of his spectacular banana crème pies or chocolate mousse cakes. I think about the many times that I myself have stood in front of his closed diner and eyed with longing the pastries that lay uneaten in the illuminated case—and I conclude that a man capable of such cruelty would surely refuse to serve these homosexual women. A fury rises within me, the fury that results when a man of great talent denies the world the pleasure of enjoying this great talent—the selfishness, the failure to understand that an individual's godly gifts are not his alone, but rather his to share with the world around him. I look at my hands, which tremble in rage. What if Michelangelo had denied us his work? Balzac? Tolstoy? Jane Austen? How might the world be harmed if the creators of beauty confined their works to the most private galleries? I am infuriated by Stavros, by his refusal to abide by this social compact, by the selfishness with which he withholds that which should be shared and shared freely.

I rise to my feet and, like a Bolshevik outside the Kremlin, shake my fist. "Guilty!" I yell. "Stavros is guilty as charged!"

The judge frowns and cracks a gavel to the desk. "What are you *doing*?" he demands, clearly infuriated by my outburst. "The trial hasn't even started yet!" He again runs a hand through his wild, silver mane. "Bailiff," he calls out, exasperated.

In my limited experience, civil servants are not known for their sense of urgency, but in this case the bailiff runs to me with the speed of a hungry puma. He places his hand on my elbow and escorts me out of the courtroom of the Honorable Ambrose Felice, through the lobby, and out to the street.

"You're excused from jury duty," he says. "*Permanently* excused." With a disgusted shake of the head, he returns to the building, turning at the last moment to glare at me.

I stand on the steps of this great institution, and my spirits are deflated. I am distraught over my impulsivity, over my inability to contain my emotions at the very moment when their containment was critical. I think about my father's sage advice to me: *The man who rules his emotions is the man who rules the world.* I sit down on the steps and think about my self-defeating behavior, my failure yet again to adhere to a societal norm, how I have not been chosen for the jury—*a jury of my peers*. So strong is my desire to be among my peers that my exclusion has left me crushed, disconnected, alone. What's the use, I think, if a man cannot be among his peers? What is such a man to do? Shall he wander this planet alone, untethered, afraid? My thoughts turn to my compatriots who might be chosen for the jury. Will it be the woman with the tuft of hair sprouting from her chin? The one in the stained shirt? Oh how I want to be seated among them, to deliberate over the fate of another human being. My eyes swell with tears, and I feel as though I may weep.

Just then, a young woman—one I recognize from the jury pool—places her hand on my shoulder. "Are you okay?" she asks.

I look up at this woman, an attractive woman of an indeterminate age. Twenty? Twenty-five? Thirty? I do not know. She has a doughy, cherubic face that projects the most profound kindness, yet there is something in her eyes—maybe the flicker of green or the enormous, white canvas beneath—that gives her an eager, agitated look and indicates an intolerance for nonsense.

"They kicked me out, too," she says with a pride that confuses me. "That guy's guilty. Guilty as fuck." I am shocked by her use of profanity, so unaccustomed am I to hearing such words spring from a woman's lips. "If a couple of dykes want a cake," she continues, "you give them a cake. Simple as that. You don't get to choose based on who a chick fucks. Right?"

I examine her face, one that projects the most resolute confidence. "Right," I say. I think about the risk to society of denying lesbians cake, and my thoughts turn to my father's argument about the slippery slope. Kingsley Walser was a man who saw the gravest danger in increments, a man who feared that just the tiniest step toward injustice was the beginning of a long, inexorable march that would end in the violation of our most sacred civil rights. "What seems small," he once told me, "may very well end up stripping you of your freedom." I think about the slippery slope in the context of the foul Stavros. What if instead of making the most delicious pastries, the Greek repaired cars? And what if he refused to fix the car of a lesbian? And what if that same lesbian required a functioning vehicle to bring medicine to her ailing mother? And could Stavros's refusal to fix her car lead to the death of this caring lesbian's mother? Or what if Stavros was instead a doctor? (Given his incomprehensible idiocy, this hypothetical is impossible.) In such an event, could he refuse to treat an ailing lesbian? I have no doubt how my father would rule. *Guilty as charged!*

The woman extends her hand to me, and after a moment's hesitation I reach out and shake it. Our hands clasped, she examines my face.

"What's wrong?" she asks. "You upset?"

I am a man of discretion and restraint, loath to share my feelings with strangers. But something about her interest in me and her support for my legal position compels me to be forthcoming.

"Yes, I am. Quite upset, in fact, as it was my hope that I would be chosen today for a jury. It would have been a great honor, of course."

The woman smirks with something akin to pity. "A great honor? It's nothing like that. Nothing more than a waste of fucking time, actually."

With the flesh beneath my left thumb, I wipe the moisture from my eyes. "Well … well …" I stammer.

She waits for me to complete my sentence. After a few silent, awkward moments, she says, "Well, good seeing you. And keep fighting the good fight."

"I shall," I say, feigning confidence. "I shall keep fighting this good fight." I do not know what good fight I might be fighting.

The woman smiles as if she has encountered a kindred spirit. "Cool," she says and runs down the front steps of the courthouse, the hem of her long skirt bobbing like a pony's tail.

As if I suffer from the most advanced rheumatoid arthritis (I do not), I stand stiffly and begin my walk toward the subway. During my short, defeated trip to the station I feel disconnected from the world around me, in shock from both the wounds of my rejection and my role in that rejection. Sounds are muffled, images blurred, smells blunted and rendered neutral. I walk, for example, through a moist cloud that emanates from the grill of a Halal truck but, inhaling deeply, smell nothing. When I reach the steps that lead down to the station, I look up to the crisp blue sky and am staggered by a fear that I will never again see its great beauty—a fear not that beauty will cease to exist, but that beauty will continue to thrive and that I shall be deprived of my ability to appreciate it.

"Move it!" screams an old woman who follows her bark with a kick to the back of my calf. "Move it!"

I turn to see a tiny woman with the most terrifying face, and although she is unimposing from a physical standpoint, I find myself intimidated by her. I shiver at the sight of her, at the confidence with which she disregards even the most basic rules of human civility. I think about the power that results from an enraged appearance and how the weak can intimidate the strong through nothing more than optics and trickery. I think about the wild animals that engage in similar chicanery—the Hemeroplanes caterpillar, which mimics a fearsome snake, for instance—compensating for their lack of menace by creating the *impression* of menace.

"Sorry," I say and limp into the current of humanity that carries me into the abyss.

On the ride home, there are numerous empty seats in the car, and I take one close to the doors. But mere seconds after the train starts, I think of the two old men from Hell's Kitchen and, aspiring to reach their age and to do so with their acute faculties, I curse my sloth and stand. With my hand on the oily pole (I remind myself to wash my hands the moment I return to my flat), I look at the other riders. A man with the craggy face of an ancient soothsayer returns my glance. He winks knowingly, and I wonder if he is somehow aware that I have been expelled from the jury. Uncomfortable, I turn away from this man with the probing gaze.

The train stops at 72nd Street, and I trudge upward to street level. In the plaza that surrounds the station, I am met with mostly familiar sights: a few homeless men attempt to sleep on benches cruelly designed to prevent their slumber; across the intersection, silly people gather eagerly in front of the hot dog and papaya stand seeking the most vile delivery mechanisms for salt, fat, and sugar; the slick salesman from the mattress store approaches the station and screams loudly into his phone. I recoil in disgust at this man and everything he represents: flash, avarice, and the destruction of our cherished neighborhood merchant.

As I turn west to continue my journey home, I notice several workers installing something in the plaza. A crowd gathers around them, and it seems to me that an event of great importance is occurring. Intrigued as always by what intrigues others, I join this crowd of onlookers and watch as the workers assemble what appears to be the base of some giant sculpture. This base, made of black metal, resembles an inverted *V*.

I turn to the woman who stands beside me. "Might you know what these men are doing? What they are constructing?"

Without answering me, she points to a sign several feet away. I thank her, then walk to this sign and see that it contains an artist's rendering of the thing being built. According to the drawing, the structure—a work of art, apparently—will when completed resemble what looks like an upside-down *Y* or a body with neither head nor arms.

I examine the shape and lines of this creation and think immediately of the font Helvetica, as the form of this thing is thick and clean like the ubiquitous sans serif font—and when I think of this lauded font, my resentment boils as it does for the bed salesman, for is there a greater symbol of the standardization and the destruction of the idiosyncratic than Helvetica? Why must we slavishly conform to a visual construct hatched in some Swiss laboratory in the middle of the twentieth century? Are there not more attractive fonts from centuries past? And are there not other, more compelling ways in which modern man can present the written word? Something that with pride contains the tiniest imperfection? Something that offers us the glorious imperfection of the artisan?

I continue on my way, taking with me a sense of dread at the completion of this installation and its potential impact on the psyche of our community. But maybe I overreact, as my father once told me I am prone to do. Perhaps I shall be surprised; perhaps this sculpture's final form will diverge from its rendering and inspire with its beauty, its design, its power. *Perhaps.*

Once home, I wash my hands, cleansing myself of whatever repugnant bacteria had coated the unhygienic subway pole, then proceed to my wardrobe. There, I begin the process of disrobing: the removal of my jacket, my cuff links, the careful untying of the silk cravat, and the unbuttoning and removal of my linen shirt, which is still damp from the perspiration of my judge-induced anxiety. I stand now before the full-length mirror dressed only in my boxer shorts and my black socks. I observe my body reflected before me and am alarmed by my weight, by my thinness, by the rows of ribs that push through my thin skin like scorching wires. I turn to the side and observe my posture, which reveals a slump of the shoulders and a distension of the gut that suggests a profound diffidence.

I again face the mirror and think not of my father's strong body—his upright stance, his flat stomach, his ropy arms—but rather of my lovely mother, whose flawed body I seem to have inherited. I picture her slumped shoulders and her drooping paunch, her sad face painted with the stress of ineluctable fears. I laugh at the recollection of her silly airs and pretenses, her head aloft in the puffy clouds. I recall those agonizing final weeks, when we could not persuade my dear depressed mother to leave her bed, when I—a young boy—made her breakfast and brought it to her on a sterling silver tray, hoping (praying, really) to lift her spirits, only to return an hour later to find the food uneaten and my troubled mother fast asleep with the blinds drawn.

I turn and again observe my profile. I straighten my spine and pull my shoulders back. I suck in my stomach and admire myself in the mirror. For a moment I feel empowered, willing to meet even the greatest physical challenge, but then my thoughts turn to the jury and my humiliating failure to fulfill my civic duty. I think about the charlatan Kilkenny and the intolerant Stavros and that spirited girl on the courthouse steps. "Guilty as fuck," she'd said. "Guilty as fuck." And I wonder what it would feel like to be so uninhibited that I could utter such words, and to do so without fear of rejection or arrest or societal scorn. I wonder why I am not free—why I have *never* been free.

My thoughts turn again to my beloved mother. I picture the heavy mass of her body hanging from the ceiling pipe, the rope around her neck—and the bucket she kicked to the bathroom floor in her final voluntary act. I exhale. I release my shoulders and slump forward. I appear to inhabit another body—my dead mother's, perhaps? And I wonder if the same tragic fate awaits me. I wonder if I am too much like her.

Three

A week has passed since my ignominious ejection from the courthouse, and my wounds are still deep and open, exposed to the city's acrid air, filled with a bitter, existential pus, a toxic fluid that courses through my veins. I once met a man—a wry, self-deprecating poet prone to bon mots and spiritual frustrations—who said "I'm living in the moment—just not this one." And he said so with a diabolical chuckle, as if his penchant for existing only in the past or in the future was cause for amusement, as if the very idea of living in the present moment was a human impossibility akin to being invisible or traveling through time or eating rich pastries without gaining weight.

Today, I too am living in the past, prone to replaying my courthouse gaffe and then revising history as a salve for my pain. (I imagine myself arguing *mens rea* and *actus reus* with such deftness that the Honorable Ambrose Felice bows to me with a deference reserved for only the greatest legal minds.) My disconsolate mood is exacerbated by a financial situation that worsens with each passing month. I have, for the past decade, lived primarily off the estate left to me by my father upon his death. With the occasional recompense for a short story or a travel essay, I have modestly augmented my inheritance, thus prolonging its existence and ameliorating the sting that often results from living a life off of assets unearned. But given the infrequency of my publication and my inability to generate meaningful revenue through the written word, my inheritance—once comfortable—has dwindled to a pitiable amount.

I call my literary agent, a woman of vigor and irrepressible spirit, who has for many years served as my greatest—and at times *only*—advocate.

"Belinda," I say, "might you give me an update on the status of my submission to the esteemed literary journal in Medicine Hat, Alberta?" I am, of course, aware that such a journal pays only the most modest amounts for a short story—three hundred dollars at most—and that any such amount would not solve my financial problems. I am told, however, that publication in a highly regarded journal often attracts the attention of editors at the largest and most prestigious publishing houses—and it is this attention that might lead to a considerable advance for the novel over which I have been toiling for years.

"Robert," she responds solemnly. "I'm afraid they've turned it down. They thought the story line was original—a brilliant Dutch counterfeiter who cares for his feeble-minded sister—but the editor felt it lacked verve—a certain *verve* they're looking for." She pauses, I assume, to allow me to process this devastating news. "Can you do that, Robert? Can you rewrite the story with more verve?"

I run a chamois over a tarnished silver stein and wonder if I am capable of more verve. "I believe I can," I say with little confidence. "I believe that I can write with more verve."

Deflated and disinclined to revising my story to meet the irrational whims of this amateurish editor from a third-rate journal, I instead turn to the morning newspaper and survey the events of the day. There are of course many wars raging throughout this complicated world—proxy wars and tribal wars, drug wars and even the most picayune squabbles between what seem to be the friendliest nation-states. The stock market appears to be fully valued—or so says a leading economist—and inflation is expected to be high (according to this same economist) or low (according to another pundit of equally impressive pedigree).

Mistrustful of the newspaper's weather predictions, I open the window and extend my arm through the aperture, attempting to glean from the temperature, the wind, and the strength of the sun what type of clothing would be most appropriate. The weather appears to be temperate, and I thus resolve to put on a pair of khaki pants, a collared shirt, and a V-neck sweater. Given my rejection from that terrible journal in Alberta (one staffed by the most hopeless fools), I do not feel particularly confident about my writing today, so I decide to take a short break from my work and instead enjoy the beauty of this day.

I step out of my building and admire the glittering world around me. How joyous and innocent are the little children and the puppies who frolic under the verdant canopy of Riverside Park. And there, circled around these very children and puppies, are the armies of Filipina and West Indian women who care for these delightful creatures. How selfless these woman are, how committed they are to the wellbeing of their charges. My own heart now warmed by what I see before me, I wave adieu to this group of caretakers, but so focused are they on the children and the mischievous puppies that they do not see me. I shrug my shoulders in admiration of their professionalism and good nature, and I walk toward Central Park, where I shall take a stroll through Olmsted's pastoral masterpiece.

To reach the park, I walk down 72nd Street, past the establishments with which I have become so familiar. First, of course, is Stavros's restaurant—which this morning is open! And what a rare occurrence it is—as rare as a volcanic explosion at Krakatoa. Through the greasy window, I see Stavros standing behind the counter. What I have recently learned from my neighbor, Dame Vivian Wanamaker—a glamorous centenarian, a Ziegfeld girl, sometimes Hindu, sometimes Buddhist—is that the intolerant Stavros pleaded *nolo contendere* to the most minor charge against him. And in exchange for this plea of no contest in the courtroom of the Honorable Ambrose Felice, a fine of one thousand dollars was levied upon him, coupled with his commitment to produce delicious pastries and cakes for no fewer than five gay or lesbian weddings.

I stand before the restaurant's window and notice that Stavros has surrendered his look of condescending judgment and instead speaks gaily with two men. They are handsome men, young and fit, who wear tank tops and shorts and have nary a hair on their muscled bodies.

These customers sit side by side at the counter, and in their outside hands—left for one, right for the other—they hold forks bearing small mountains of what I know to be the most delicious red velvet cake. I look and see that their free hands are clasped tightly. I look to Stavros, who leans forward, elbows on the counter, and smiles so sincerely that I cannot believe what I am seeing. He makes an encouraging motion with his hands, does Stavros, and the two hand-holding men simultaneously place their forks in their mouths and eat the moist red velvet cake. After a few thoughtful chews, the two men raise their empty forks in triumph and nod approvingly—a validation that causes Stavros to leap like a circus seal and clap his hands in delight.

I take two steps toward the window, so that I am now just inches from the glass. From this perspective, I have a better view of the scene before me and can confirm that a transformation has occurred in Stavros, some shift from deep within that has altered the way this man sees and experiences the world. What I sense in him is some cracking open, as if the stress of indictment and near incarceration has had an illuminative effect on him, as if his brush with the blunt force of the law has caused a realignment of his values.

I believe that Stavros is now eager to shed his selfish snakeskin, eager to at last share his God-given gifts with the entire world—homosexuals included. And as he refills the coffee cups of these two fit men, he smiles with affection, a further indication that he possesses both the capacity and the willingness to change. Oh how uplifted I am, how encouraged by this evolution, for it offers me hope that even the most obstinate man—a man like

Polsky or even the myopic editor from the Alberta journal—is capable of self-examination and change.

Pleased with what I have just witnessed, I continue along 72nd Street and approach the plaza that surrounds the subway station. A team of workers continues to construct the great metal sculpture, and I pause to review their progress and to assess the artistic merit of this enormous structure. The inverted *V* is now anchored to the pavement with bolted panels, its peak a good thirty feet off the ground. I look up and marvel at its size, its thickness, its inky color—all ominous in a manner that suggests some sort of industrial brutality. I take a step toward this inert creature, and this movement causes its impenetrable mass to block the sun, casting me in a cool, deathly shadow.

As if I am being devoured by some giant beast, I experience a crushing sensation in my gut and struggle to breathe. I tremble in fear and, seeking relief, quickly dart back into the warm sun, which has a therapeutic effect and restores my physiology to normalcy. Shielding my eyes from the light, I look up to this partially constructed thing and see a worker ascending a ladder with an armful of wires and cords, switches, and other assorted electronic equipment. When he reaches the top of the ladder, he is positioned just above the incomplete structure—above the peak of this inverted *V*—and after looking down into the emptiness of this monstrosity, he carefully lowers this bundle of wires, cords and switches—these electronic entrails—into the sculpture's dark cavern.

Satisfied that he has completed his task, the worker descends the ladder one carefully taken step at a time and, once on the ground, joins his co-workers. There, the men stand in a straight line and gaze up at this thing they are assembling. Then, after wiping their brows in unison, they turn to a nearby table and review what appears to be the engineering plans that guide their efforts.

I wonder when this sculpture will be completed, how tall it will be—how I will feel about it. (I hope it will fit proportionately into the dimensions of our quaint neighborhood.) I wonder, what is the purpose of these wires, these cords and switches? With these irksome questions filling my mind, I turn away—toward the park, toward nature and the beauty that awaits. But as I continue eastward, as I am about to reach that nefarious purveyor of mass-produced bedding, that symbol of the corrosive acid that is globalization, I notice a woman—a girl, really. I gasp, for this girl is the spitting image of Rose!

Now, I cannot say such a thing for sure, as I have never actually met my red-breasted robin nor seen a photograph or painting of her. I have, however, been blessed with numerous letters from her, the most desperate missives that convey the horrors of a life gone astray. And it is through these letters, through the grace with which Rose faces the darkest forces, that I have conjured a mental image of her.

And it is this mental image, so clear and crisp, that somehow has found life through this very girl—a delicate, pale flower who now stands before me and peers quizzically through the window of the vulgar bed store. She is just as I had envisioned—of medium height, but thin, almost frail, as if deprived of nutrition either through penury or a loss of appetite resulting from the most cosmic struggles. Her hair is the darkest black, and one might assume that she has dyed it, for there is not a single strand of brown or auburn; her skin, so pale and unblemished, resembles the pristine surface of the finest bone china; her green eyes flicker with the fiery resolve of the oppressed; and she smiles the weary smile of one who knows that true justice is a fallacy, that the great forces of commerce and legacy and inheritance and tenure (judicial, academic, and otherwise) are far too powerful to be overcome by mere generosity of spirit.

I am now so convinced that Rose stands before me that I call out to her. "Rose!" I exclaim warmly.

The girl turns and looks at me. "Excuse me?" she says.

I remove my cap from my head. "Might you be Rose? Rose of Philadelphia?"

As if she fears that I might mug her, the girl reaches for her purse and clutches it close to her chest. "I'm not Rose," she says. "I'm— I'm— I'm somebody else." She leans forward, toward me, and examines me as if she is trying to determine if I am friend or foe. "And I've never been to Philadelphia," she assures me.

I roll the cap in my hands. "Of course," I reply. "Of course you are not Rose." I turn and look through the window and into the showroom. Inside, the oily salesman who accosted me earlier shows a mattress to the most clueless mark. The salesman pats the mattress with his hand, an invitation for the customer to test what surely is a product constructed of reused and toxic materials. "Are you looking for a bed?" I ask the girl, eyeing the family-owned store across the street.

Having already made a decision about my friend-foe status, it appears, the girl withdraws and takes a purposeful step away from me. "No," she says. "I already have a bed. A perfectly good bed."

I experience a hot flush on my cheeks, an indication that they have turned a beet red and have announced my mortification. I again curse my foolishness, my tendency—dating back to my childhood—to see everywhere signs of benevolence, only to be met with the harsh reality of a cruel world. How, I wonder, could I be so foolish as to think that my beloved Rose had finally come to me, that I had through some miracle stumbled upon her in front of the mattress store, that her physical appearance would so closely comport with my mental image. And how could I be so foolish as to believe that I might be loved by this woman—by *any* woman, really—one who would overlook what I sometimes fear may be a set of traits and characteristics, *philosophies* even, that are not fit for this world. ("You are a tragic man, Walser, one who suffers from generational dysmorphia," Polsky once said to me at an English Department cocktail party—and he did so to the cruel delight of a gaggle of intoxicated academics.)

The girl smiles at me with a look that carries hints of pity and fear. She turns east, and I watch as she walks toward the park. I watch not in the prurient way that a construction worker might stare at the posterior of a Rubenesque woman, but in the way that a man observes irrefutable evidence of his own failings.

Terrified by the possibility of a life spent in solitude, I turn back—away from this girl, away from the park—and I wonder who might love me. I wonder if, despite my best intentions and a spirit that my father often described as too trusting, I am destined to live in a state of separation from the world around me. Rather than continue toward the park, I walk west down 72nd Street, back toward my apartment. I pass a hardware store, and in my peripheral vision something in the window catches my attention. I pause and observe in the shop window a collection of saws and mops, pumps and tools, none of which I find remarkable, none of which is the cause of my curiosity. But then I see something in the corner of the window: a still life of sorts—a sad still life. My heart races, and it does so with thoughts of my dear mother, my tragic mother—for there, glowing under a column of the most tawdry fluorescent light, is a thick rope draped over a metal bucket.

I gasp for air, so overcome am I by grief. Perspiration covers my brow and hot saliva fills my mouth. I stare again at the rope and the bucket, and I recall with unspeakable grief the circular swoop of her body as it—as *she*—hung lifeless from the ceiling pipe. As I divert my gaze from the shop window, I recall my father's frantic attempt to cut the rope.

"Hold her! Hold her up!" he screamed to me as he stood up on the toilet with a knife in hand. I put my arms around her waist and pushed up onto my toes, reducing the tension of the rope and its pressure on my mother's neck. Struggling to support the weight of her body, I looked up to see my father sawing through the rope with a steak knife, tears running down his cheeks. "No, no!" he howled. "No!"

The rope finally popped, and my mother fell down— down into my arms—so heavy that we both crashed to the floor. Still clutching her waist, I lay on the cold tile with the full weight of my dead mother on top of me.

I again stare at the rope and the bucket in the window. I gather the saliva in my mouth and, with a rage long suppressed, spit at the glass. I pause to watch the froth run down the shiny surface and obscure this image that so pains me. And before anyone can object to my transgression, before anyone can bear witness to this grotesque act, I sprint west, past the monstrous sculpture, toward the dreadful river—whitecaps dotting an awful battleship grey.

Four

This morning I am filled with a sense of nervous anticipation, for today I am scheduled to attend a job interview
with an advertising agency, one that I am told is highly
regarded for its cleverness and its ability to generate
demand for the most diverse range of consumer products.
This interview was arranged by my loyal agent, Belinda St.
Clair, who fears that my financial predicament has become
so dire that my ability to write may become impaired. I am
scheduled to meet with this preeminent agency's creative
director: Belinda's grand-nephew and a man with whom I
shall discuss the possibility of my becoming a copywriter.

Given the importance of this meeting, I dress in my
finest attire: the same suit I wore to jury duty, a pale blue
Egyptian cotton shirt, and, instead of the grey cravat I
wore to the courthouse, a burgundy bowtie with a delicate
crepe texture. I admire myself in the full-length mirror,
impressed now by my posture and an unusual confidence
that emanates from deep within.

As I turn side to side, I imagine my dialogue with this creative director, how I shall impress him with clever jingles that I conjure extemporaneously. (*Perrier, the perfect way to make your day! Perrier, the drink that makes your mood so gay!*) I picture the man, a look of astonishment on his face. "You *just* thought that up?" he says, shocked by my ability to so quickly capture the essence of a product. "I did," I reply with a modesty that we both know is unwarranted.

With my customary punctuality, I arrive fifteen minutes early at the agency's Madison Avenue offices. There, I introduce myself by my full name—Robert Kingsley Walser—to a receptionist who is blessed with the most impeccable style. She is dressed in a simple black sleeveless dress (the most sophisticated women in this city always seem to dress in black), and around her neck hangs a strand of black Tahitian pearls, each one the size of a blueberry. Her blonde hair is pulled back in a ponytail that is held not by an elastic band, but by a Victorian barrette with a shimmering layer of diamonds. In each ear is the simplest platinum post. After hearing my name, she smiles (an indication, perhaps, that my arrival is highly anticipated). She rises and leads me to the room where I shall meet the creative director, and as I follow her down the hallway I try in a gentlemanly way not to observe the subtle sway of her hips and the red-soled shoes that must have cost a considerable sum.

She exudes such prosperous confidence, this woman, that my thoughts turn to Rose—not because she and this woman are similar, but because they could not be more dissimilar. Where this woman is swaddled in a cloak of the most supreme assurance and contentment, Rose is encased in a flurry of traumas and challenges, obstacles and privations. I wonder, as I often do, about the many forces beyond effort, scholarship, and good intention that guide a person's life: genetics, inheritance, upbringing, Providence, and the like.

This fortunate woman leads me to a conference room, a bright, sunny room on the corner that is decorated with what I understand to be iconic mid-century pieces by such luminaries as Saarinen, Breuer, Jacobsen, and Le Corbusier. This popular décor has always been too stark and minimal for my traditional aesthetic (I tend toward the gold-leafed, the tufted, the antiquated), but I do carry an appreciation for these clean, simple designs and for the quality of the materials and workmanship employed in their creation—a rare appreciation for an otherwise ignoble twentieth century. Still, these popular designs have approached universality and—at least for me—thus carry with them some of the brute efficiency of the font Helvetica. The woman leads me to an orange chair that resembles a large half-egg and, her hand on my elbow, she guides me down and into the chair.

As if I am a fledgling awaiting a worm from my mother's beak, I look up at this woman and lick my dry lips. "If it is not too much of an imposition, might I bother you for a glass of water?"

"Of course," she says, and from a nearby cabinet withdraws a bottle of water. She unscrews the top (how thoughtful) and hands the bottle to me. "Mister St. Clair will be in shortly," she says and then withdraws. Alone in the room, I put the plastic bottle to my lips and take a sip. I examine the bottle, holding it up to the natural light that streams through the south-facing windows. I place the bottle on a side table, and my thoughts turn to my mother, a particular woman who abhorred casualness when it came to hospitality; regardless of the event (Christmas dinner or a summer barbeque), she served drinks in fine crystal and food on bone china—and she made no apologies for her fussiness.

The door opens and in walks Bernard St. Clair, a manila folder in one hand. In appearance, he is not like what I had imagined. The mental image that I had constructed of this creative director was one consistent, I now concede, with an era long gone. Rather than sporting the finely cut suit and pomaded hair of an old adman, St. Clair instead resembles a radical of some sort—an anarchist, a nihilist, I do not know. He wears a black T-shirt on which is painted a terrifying face: it is the face of a pale white man with a disgusted scowl and a mop of spiked black hair. Near the top of the shirt are painted the words *Sid Vicious*, and below, the words *Gimme a Fix*. I wonder who this Sid Vicious is—a cartoon character, a villain in a movie?—and why his face is on a T-shirt. Either way, this attire strikes me as inappropriate for a serious work environment, especially within a firm so highly regarded. On St. Clair's face is an untrimmed moustache and a scruffy chin patch, giving him a look reminiscent of a fiery Trotsky.

St. Clair approaches me and extends his hand. "Bobby," he says, using the diminutive of my name—a presumptuous familiarity. I lean forward and try to stand, only to fall back into the strange egg chair. I try pushing up with my right arm, which causes an imbalance in the chair that I fear may result in a capsizing event, with both me and the chair crashing to the floor. I fall back into the chair. "Don't bother," St. Clair says with a hint of amusement, "no need to get up."

I am relieved and shake his hand. From his lofty perch, he squeezes so tightly that I wonder if he is trying to make a point—and what that point might be. He sits down in an identical egg chair a few feet away.

"Oh," he exclaims. "A *water*." Without even the slightest effort, he leaps from the chair, and I wonder if he studied ballet as a child. "You good?" he asks, pointing toward my bottle.

"I'm good," I reply, mimicking his vernacular.

The creative director removes a bottle of water from the cabinet and returns to his chair. "Thanks for coming by," he says. He pauses and studies me the way an entomologist might study a rare bug. "I guess no one told you we're casual here. *Creative*'s casual, at least. Accounting and legal, not so much."

I look down at my suit, at my antique cuff links, at my loafers. I tug gently on my burgundy bowtie. I curse myself for not having worn my chinos, my button-down shirt, and a cashmere sweater; I curse my propensity to so often dress more formally than circumstances dictate and wonder if my dress might have the effect of creating a barrier between me and others.

"Well," he continues, "Belinda says a lot of great things about you."

My chest swells with the pride of the complimented. "That's quite kind of her."

St. Clair opens the manila folder and flips through several papers. "She sent me some writing samples." He holds up a piece of paper. "One of your short stories, I guess." He waves the paper as if he is using a Japanese folding fan on a muggy day. "This one was— This one was—" I await his verdict. "This one was *interesting*."

I exhale in relief, although I do not know to which story he refers. "Thank you for your kind words, sir. Might I ask which story you find interesting?"

He leans forward and turns the page in my direction so that I can see for myself. "The Dutch guy," he says. "The Dutch counterfeiter who's screwing his retarded sister."

I gasp in horror.

"That's dark. That's *really* dark," he continues. "Edgy and dark, and the sort of way we think about things here— how we think about advertising. We push limits." He returns the paper to the folder and takes a sip of water.

I try to maintain my composure. I am outraged by the disrespect that he shows—not to my writing (because that is just writing, after all), but to my *characters*, to my brilliant and loving Lars and to his damaged sister, Lieke. How dare he impugn their fine values, their pure intentions, their kind hearts! I am outraged by St. Clair's profanity, how he has suggested that the complex relationship between Lars and Lieke is sexual in nature— which it most certainly is not.

I am a gentle man, but I am a man of principle—and when my most deeply cherished principles have been offended, I defend them without fear of consequence. (That is what my dear father taught me: to defend one's principles *without fear of consequence*.) As if propelled by some great volcanic force below, I leap out of the egg chair and stand before and above this anarchist, this nihilist. (Given his comment about Lars and Lieke, I now think it most likely that he is a nihilist.)

"Lars," I declare, "is a man of the very highest character, and—"

"He's a counterfeiter!" St. Clair interjects smugly.

I squeeze the plastic bottle, causing the water to spurt over the sides and splash to the floor below. "He uses the counterfeit loot for the most noble purposes: to assist the poor and to undermine the currency of a wicked king with the goal of toppling said king," I counter with the outrage of the falsely accused. "And he is not scr— scr—"

I cannot say the word, for to do so would somehow grant legitimacy to St. Clair's vile interpretation. "He is not romantically intimate with his sister. He is— He is—"

"Sleeping in bed with her," he shouts.

A dark cloud passes over the sun and darkens the office—and I am exasperated by an idiocy that rivals that of Stavros. "She has *nightmares* if she sleeps alone," I say. "He does it to bring Lieke comfort—to allow her the pleasure of a night's sound sleep."

St. Clair stands and takes a step toward me in an aggressive manner. "And what about *bathing* her?" he says accusingly. "Hands all over her!"

To question the integrity of Lars—my great creation—is to question the power of the Titans; to assign an incestuous motive to Lars is, I believe, the greatest of insults. I place the bottle of water on a side table and gather my thoughts. If we were not living in this modern century, I would have no choice but to challenge St. Clair to a duel—in Weehawken, perhaps, at the foot of the Palisades. But sadly, we live in a time that does not tolerate such a dignified resolution to conflict, so I instead decide to correct his misunderstanding.

"Given her disability, Lieke cannot bathe herself, so

Lars takes it upon himself to clean his sister in the most tender and respectful manner."

St. Clair looks at me with condescension.

"And in doing so," I continue, "there are moments when his hands come into contact with certain parts of her body and, under different circumstances, that contact might be deemed intimate or suggestive of some amorous intent. But under these circumstances his behavior is irrefutable evidence of a boundless and pure love for his disabled sister."

St. Clair retreats several steps and gazes out the window. "So all that was sincere? You weren't being ironic?"

I ponder the absurdity of his thinking. "Ironic! Of course not. There is not the tiniest shred of irony in the whole story—or in any of my stories, for that matter."

The man laughs for some unexplained reason, then turns back to me and winks—the type of smarmy wink that the bed salesman might give an unsuspecting customer. "Check," he says. We are not playing chess, so I am unsure why he has said such a thing. He crosses the room and tosses the manila folder onto a table. "Sorry, but I don't think we've got a fit here." He extends his hand, which I eye with some trepidation before extending my own. But unlike the excessive squeeze of moments ago, his grip is now weak and flaccid. "But send my regards to Belinda," he says—a threat or a conciliation, I do not know.

And before I can utter a single word, St. Clair is gone. I stand alone in the conference room. I look around at the austere yet iconic furniture and wonder what has become of this world. I look outside, at the clear blue sky that is denied its rightful brilliance by one stubborn cloud that blocks the sun. I approach the window and look up at this stubborn cloud, and then I blow at it as if I am blowing the cottony bloom from a dandelion. And as if my lungs expel the gale-force winds of the gods, the cloud darts away from the sun, restoring an azure to the sky and again bathing the room in the most brilliant light. I hold my face up to the sun and allow the warmth to sear my cheeks. I look around at the expensive furniture and wonder about my finances—what I might do to earn an income, how a man like me might earn a reasonable wage in this fast and unforgiving world.

The door to the conference room opens, and the fortunate woman enters. She stands before me, arms crossed over her chest in a manner that conveys defiance. "I'm happy to show you out," she says, with little of her earlier graciousness. She spins as if atop a turntable and walks out of the room with an imperious authority. I dutifully follow (for what else can I do?), and as we walk toward the elevator, I am careful not to glance at the sway of her hips, focusing instead on her red-soled shoes. She turns to the right, and when she does so, I notice a slight tear in the leather of her shoe—an imperfection that has been partially covered up with a strip of black electrical tape. I glance at the barrette in her hair and notice several missing stones; and when she presses the elevator button for me, her hand reveals a torn cuticle and chipped nail polish. I reconsider this woman—and the impression that she first conveyed—and I wonder if perhaps she is not as fortunate as I had earlier assumed.

Five

🐚

I awoke yesterday to a great tragedy. At just a few minutes past six, the sounds of radios and medics filled the external hallway. I leapt from my bed and, in my pajamas, shuffled through the dark apartment to the front door. I peered through the peephole and there, in the distorting glass, I saw the most horrible sight: Dame Vivian Wanamaker being pushed on a stretcher. The centenarian's eyes were closed, her mouth open, and her skin a dreary pearl grey. I was concerned, of course, but what magnified my concern above all else was the lack of urgency in her transport, for she was being guided through the hall as if time were irrelevant, as if her medical condition required no immediate treatment—as if the medics were enjoying a Sunday stroll through the Tuileries. I would soon learn that my concern was justified, for the great Dame Wanamaker had died.

I sit now at my kitchen table and stare into a cage that contains the old lady's beloved hamster, Luna. This nervous rodent—with its twitching nose and its slivered eyes—was given to me by the superintendent of the building, a callous man who not only refused to care for the creature following Vivian's death, but had the audacity to suggest that the hamster be released into the wilds of Central Park. I could not bear the thought of Luna's loneliness, the horrible fate that would await her if exposed to the elements, so I offered to take in this rodent and treat her as if she were my very own child.

The hamster now stares at me with grief, and I wonder what she wants. I extend a strip of carrot into the cage; she sniffs, but does not take it in her tiny jaws. I maneuver the water bottle so that the steel tube is close to Luna's mouth. I watch as she sniffs the tube with her twitching nose and then takes a few sips of the cool water. When she finishes drinking, she winks at me, and my heart leaps with the joy of one who has given sustenance to another living creature.

To the right of the cage is Vivian's other supreme love: the most impressive bonsai, a miniaturized white pine with gnarls and twists, with rich, green foliage and bulging roots which she had tended to with the greatest care for more than thirty years. The same callous superintendent who refused to care for the hamster has also refused to tend to this old plant, and so I have taken possession of it as well. It is a remarkable thing, this bonsai, not just for its age and for its accurate mimicry of a full-sized tree, but for its therapeutic powers—the tranquility that it provided Vivian. I think about the commitment to detail—the unrecognized, unadvertised commitment to detail—of generations past; I think about how the Divine is found not only in the tiniest creations, but in those modest souls who seek no acclaim for their tiny (yet great) creations.

I turn back to Luna, who stares at me with the milky eyes of an old dog. I lean close and inhale, for she is bathed as always in the glorious, perfumed scent of Chanel No. 5—which Dame Wanamaker sprayed on her with the most caring regularity. ("A pet must never smell like a pet," she once said with a wave of the iconic glass bottle.) I step back and observe Luna. I watch as she blinks feverishly and her body starts to shake—great, rapid rotations of the body, as if she is a drenched Labrador who has just emerged from the surf. The hamster takes one jittery, unsure step in my direction and, thinking that she may be hungry, I reach for the carrot. But before I can push the carrot through the cage's bars, the precious rodent falls on her side, her tiny paws sticking out like the terrifying gargoyles of Notre-Dame. I gasp in horror and leap to my feet, wondering what might be the next right action. My father was a man who handled unexpected challenges with the greatest aplomb, and I believe I have inherited this same trait. I dash into the bathroom and pull a towel from the warmer (oh what a treat this warmer is!), then return to the kitchen and place the towel over the cage.

I hastily make my way to the elevator and out on to the street, where I am blessed with the good fortune of flagging a yellow cab the very moment I step out from under the building's canopy. I settle into the back seat of the taxi, cage by my side, and ponder my destination.

"Where to?" the driver asks.

During my many walks through the streets of the Upper West Side, I have observed hundreds of commercial enterprises and have thus created a mental map that is at all times available to me. I close my eyes and scan this mental map, one that manifests in a flashing imagery not unlike a zoetrope: in sequence, I see a bakery that serves the moistest cupcakes, an old-fashioned hardware store from which wafts an intoxicating aroma of motor oil, pine and rubber, a condiment shop that sells only olive oil and mustard (they are specialists, I suppose). Then I see in the mind's eye that for which I am searching: a painted sign on which a delightful puppy and a kitten play with a striped ball.

I picture the location of this vivid and joyful sign and the veterinarian's office that it announces. "Eighty-eighth and Broadway, please. Godspeed!"

For reasons that are unclear to me, the driver turns and looks at me with mouth agape, as if I have spoken in an indecipherable language—an African clicking language, perhaps. He shakes his head and engages the transmission, and within minutes, Luna and I are taken to the door of this animal doctor. With great haste, I run through the front door and into the office, one that teems with cats, dogs and owners of all sizes and breeds.

"We require immediate assistance," I say to the woman behind the counter and hold the toweled cage up for her to see.

"What's in there?" she asks without looking up from whatever petty, ministerial task distracts her from the emergency at hand.

"It is a hamster," I respond, panting. "I have a hamster who is ill ... *gravely* ill."

The receptionist still does not look up from whatever foolish thing she is doing. "We don't treat hamsters," she says. "You need a vet who specializes in exotic pets."

"Exotic pets?" I mumble. Such a classification brings to my mind a pink cockatoo, a fennec fox, a marmoset—a monitor lizard. I lift the towel and look at the sick rodent, which continues to lie on its side and twitch, its tiny claws clenched in tight balls. I recall the day when Vivian acquired Luna, how she regaled me with the tale of the animal's purchase. ("The hamster was three dollars...but the cage, the cedar chips and the food cost *fifty*.") "Where might I find this vet of exotic pets?" I ask the woman. Without even the granting me the decency of a glance in my direction, she hands me a card, and I wonder if this woman has spent so much time interacting with animals that she has lost the ability to relate to the most common animal of all—*the human being.*

Within moments, Luna and I are in yet another yellow cab and on the way to this vet who cares for only the rarest of pets. It is as if the gods are looking over us, for the streets are oddly free of traffic and every light turns green in honor of our arrival—and given our good fortune, we arrive at this new veterinarian's office in a matter of minutes. I enter the office, hold the cage up high and, like a magician at *the reveal*, violently snatch the towel. The woman behind the counter flinches, stands and peers into the cage. "Oh, my," she says at the sight of poor Luna and leads me with urgency to an examination room, where I place the cage on the center of a bare table. I press my nose against the thin metal bars and see that Luna still lies on her side, her tiny paws clenched in balls. From my pocket, I remove a slice of carrot. I open the door of the cage and hold the carrot in front of her dry nose, which to my horror no longer twitches.

The exotic pet veterinarian enters the room. I notice

that there is a downy, red feather on his white lab coat, and I wonder if it is the plume of a rare parrot, possibly a scarlet macaw. After a perfunctory nod in my direction, he reaches into the cage and lifts poor Luna from her bed, one that is comprised of the most fragrant cedar shavings. He cups the ailing rodent in his hands and then presses a miniscule stethoscope to Luna's chest.

"Hmm ..." the veterinarian hums in a foreboding manner.

I gaze into Luna's milky eyes. "What is it?"

He holds his finger to his lips to indicate a need for quiet. "Her ..." The vet looks between Luna's legs and confirms the poor thing's gender. "Her heart rate is slow ... too slow." He places the rodent on a scale and looks at the blinking numbers. "And she's underweight ... severely underweight."

I am no medical doctor, of course, but I do know enough about the workings of the body—human and animal—to know that a slow heart rate and emaciation suggest a dire prognosis. "And what might this lead you to conclude?" I ask.

Blessed soul, the doctor drapes a soft chamois cloth over Luna to keep her warm. "I'm afraid her prognosis isn't good. She's got only hours to live."

I gasp, for the likelihood of Luna's demise so soon after Vivian's death reminds me of my own beloved parents—how my vital, healthy father fell into the very depths of despair following my mother's suicide, how his physical and mental conditions deteriorated at an incomprehensible rate, how he was dead eighteen months to the day after we found my dear mother hanging from the bathroom ceiling. I recall the months after my father passed, when I first buckled under the existential weight of my own solitude—when I understood that I was alone in the world, untethered, and might be so forever.

"Hours?" I say.

The doctor nods gravely. "You should consider putting her to sleep."

"Sleep?"

The doctor notices the scarlet feather on the lapel of his white lab coat. He removes it, smiles as if he is reminded of a pleasant memory and then blows on the feather, causing it to float lazily through the air and settle on the floor below. "Yes," he says, "euthanasia."

It is this word—*euthanasia*—that evokes in me a distinct childhood memory. We had a beautiful Airedale named Ophelia, an excitable, loving terrier who gave birth to four puppies: three were the most healthy and confident creatures, but one was deeply troubled from the moment of her conception. My father and I had just returned from church and were in the back barn of our New Hope property as Ophelia gave birth to these puppies, as she licked the placenta from each one, removing this protective layer, exposing them to this great world, freeing them to breathe the sweet nectar of the Bucks County air.

The last of the four was half the size of the others and possessed not one, but two legs that were terribly deformed. My father groaned and shook his head at the sight of this runt. "This one ..." he said, not finishing his thought. He walked to the other side of the barn and, with a hose, filled a bucket. He then returned to Ophelia and her litter. He bent down and removed the runt, pulling the puppy away from her mother. With a gaze that bespoke the greatest understanding of what was about to happen, Ophelia looked up at my father, and I swear that I saw a tear form in her eye. She squealed as if she were suffering some great wound and, unable to watch, turned her attention back to her remaining puppies. My pained father grimaced and stood over the bucket. I watched as he mouthed words that I could not hear—was it a prayer?—and then dropped the runt into the bucket. Stunned, I ran to the bucket. I looked down and saw the puppy floating dead in the water below.

"Euthanasia," I reply to the doctor. "Yes, I think that is the most compassionate thing to do."

"Would you like to say goodbye?" the vet asks, holding Luna out to me.

I think about the drowned runt and the tear in Ophelia's eye. "Goodbye, dear Luna," I say.

An interminable hour later, I depart the exotic pet veterinarian's office with the cremated remains of the deceased rodent in a beautiful mahogany box. On top of the box is a brass plate inscribed with the name *Luna Wanamaker*. For a mere two hundred dollars, the doctor has transported Luna to the afterlife in the most gentle and painless way (a massive dose of tranquilizers, he said), cremated her in a manner that would coincide with Vivian's love for the Eastern religions, and laid the creature's cremains to rest in this beautifully wrought mini-sarcophagus. As I walk with the glistening box under my arm, I experience a rare sense of contentment—a feeling that I have nobly honored the lives (and deaths) of two important beings: Vivian and Luna Wanamaker.

I decide to walk over to Columbus and then down to 69th Street, where I shall stop in at the local shoe repair shop—a sliver of a place that is set in the narrowest alley between two buildings and is operated by a serene and skilled craftsman. (I marvel not only at a human being's ability to work so productively in such a cramped area, but at the ingenuity of those landlords who turn the most inhospitable spaces into generators of revenue.) It is my hope that this genius with all things leather will be able to repair my ostrich belt, which was passed on to me after my father's death and which now shows so much wear that I fear it will soon disintegrate.

As I walk east toward Columbus, I hear behind me a commotion. I turn to see a pack of youths engaged in some sort of disturbance, an ado marked by loud hollering and undignified profanity. With some concern, I turn and continue eastward, quickening my step to create as much distance as possible from these miscreants. I resolve not to look back in their direction, for to do so may invite some unwanted interaction, but I do listen closely for the volume of their voices, measuring the Doppler effect to determine their proximity—and it sounds to me as if they are closing in on me. I pass the steps of a charming townhouse in front of which an old woman sits. ("Good day!" I say to her with cheer. She ignores me.) I quicken my pace, as my animal instincts indicate to me that this group of boys is now just feet behind me. Their loud and frantic voices, their profanity, their primitive clan-like nature all suggest to me the possibility of some imminent harm. Still, I refuse to turn and face them for fear that I might incite them into even greater mischief.

I quicken my pace further, so that I am now cantering along at a clip to which I am not accustomed. The voices of these boys grow louder, and I can now smell their foul sweat upon me. I refuse to look back. Their steps are right upon me, and I feel something on my back—a hand, most likely—and then, without warning, am dropped by a fist to the back of my head. Luna's box slips from my hands and lands on the sidewalk, a few feet from my reach. I lie on the ground and look up at this pack of ruffians—young boys, no more than fifteen or sixteen years of age. One of them wears a T-shirt with the insignia of an exclusive private school located in the neighborhood; another wears a baseball cap with the crest of another prestigious school, this one a hill school in Riverdale. I wonder what has corrupted their privileged upbringings—what terrible force or omission has corrupted their lives. What I really want to know is how these young boys have been transformed into *monsters*.

"Why?" I ask them. I reach for Luna's box, but one of the boys—the one in the baseball cap—lifts his foot and steps on my arm.

"*Fuck* why," he says. He bends down and snatches the box.

"Please, no," I beg.

The boy tucks the box under his arm. He smiles at me with an icy malevolence, a pleasure even, and before I can say another word he and his pack are running back toward Broadway—and gone with them is Luna's box.

"No," I scream and shake a fist in their direction. "You have stolen sacred remains." I struggle to my feet. "You have taken something important to me!" Immune to my pleas, the boys continue. They toss the box among them, as though they are playing catch on the schoolyard, then turn the corner and disappear into the anonymous mob of this sometimes benevolent, often brutal city.

I weep as a rage overcomes me, a primal rage that originates in some far and distant place, from some deep, dark pocket that I have never before accessed, but which must exist within me—for here it is. I no longer wonder or theorize or imagine or speculate. *No, no!* What I feel now is the antithesis of abstract theory and concept; what I feel now is real and unmistakable, potent and powerful; what I feel now is tangible. For the first time in my life, I hate. *I hate.* And in doing so, I experience the most transcendent sense of liberation—an empowerment that comes with the most intense emotions released, dispersed, freed.

"Fuck you!" I yell to the boys—to these monsters. I take several deep, panting breaths and think about the bold woman on the courthouse steps. "Fuck you!" I yell again, but this time to my dear mother's depression...to my father's greatness...to the Titans...to every person and force—kind or malevolent—that has damaged me. I think about my neighbor Dame Vivian and about Luna and her tiny gargoyle paws, her twitching nose, the soft fur of her belly. I wonder what will become of her remains, what will become of her. And in so wondering, I seem to access yet another unknown pocket of rage, for I clench my jaws with such force that the grinding of my teeth emits a sharp, scraping sound. "Fuck you!" I howl, crushed by the most exquisite pain. "Fuck you, *Rose!*"

Six

✺

So consumed am I by the loss of Luna's ashes and the shame of my blasphemous outburst that I have not left my apartment for two days. To have betrayed Dame Vivian by failing to care for her beloved hamster is exquisitely painful. To have raged against both my mother's disease (or did I in fact rage against my mother herself?) and my father's greatness was outrageous in its offense; but to rage against Rose—poor, innocent and kind Rose—was an offense of the highest and most despicable order. After much sober reflection, I cannot explain this anger that welled up from deep within and burst forth like a solar flare. I am a gentle and forgiving man, so I am told, disinclined to critical judgment, and I thus wonder if I may have suffered some sort of brain injury when pummeled by those delinquents, a trauma to the head that for just a few minutes altered my personality in the most terrible way.

As I look out the window and watch a pinprick of a cloud dance across the sky, I decide that remaining in this isolated, homebound state is no antidote for my remorse, and I resolve to leave my apartment and stroll through the familiar and pleasing streets of my neighborhood. Two loops on my ostrich belt now hang by a mere thread, and the tip of the belt has frayed, leading to a separation of the upper and lower layers—so I shall make the shop of the serene shoe and leather repairman a destination on my stroll (a destination that was aborted after I was felled by those violent youths).

After dressing in a manner most appropriate for an afternoon walk—khakis, a cotton sweater, tennis sneakers—I descend to the lobby. There, I see Vivian Wanamaker's estranged daughter—a mean-spirited woman who had not visited her mother in many years. She is here to clean out Vivian's apartment. I wave to her, but she does not reciprocate, and I fear that her hostility indicates a desire to reclaim the bonsai. (I shall not surrender it, for I know that Dame Wanamaker would have wanted me to care for this precious mini-tree.) I dart out of the lobby before she can make such a request, firm in my belief that she is a disrespectful daughter who failed to appreciate her mother's many lovely qualities.

I walk east on 72nd Street, and to my utter amazement Stavros's restaurant is again open. I notice that now hanging from the canopy above his entrance is another one of those cheerful rainbow flags. I wonder what it is about these flags, what they mean and why they have become so common. As I pass, Stavros sees me and waves with surprising glee. I wave back, impressed that his personality seems to have changed to such a degree that he may as well be an entirely different person. This Stavros, I think, is a finer human being—a finer *citizen*—than the

Stavros of old. He is, I believe, a sparkling example of a misguided person being rehabilitated by our virtuous criminal justice system.

Ostrich belt in hand, I continue east toward the subway plaza where the sculpture is being erected. Days have passed since I last viewed this monstrosity, and I approach with great anticipation, eager to see what progress has been made. As I near Broadway, this dark metal thing towers above the scores of people who scurry like fire ants in and out of the station. I stand on the corner, fifty or so feet away from this edifice, and tremble at its recent evolution. For built atop the metal base is now a rigid extension that is twisted like a sailor's rope or the rough threads of a screw—so that the entire sculpture, at least in its present form, suggests an inverted Y of sorts with a twirled shaft.

Two oddly dressed people (they wear sandals and socks), tourists surely, stand under the sculpture's base and look upward, and it appears to me as if they are standing under the legs—under the groin—of a giant. I laugh at the folly of people, how even the most foolish things can intrigue them. The pedestrian light turns green, and I cross Broadway and move to within mere feet of this thing. I wonder about its aesthetic purpose and about the wires, switches and cords that the worker earlier lowered into its bowels. I would like to know how much such a thing cost to design and assemble so I can make a list of more useful ways this money could have been spent. (My list is typical for lists of this nature: money for schools and libraries, and care for the elderly and the infirm.)

I look over to the sign that weeks ago offered only a depiction of the sculpture. From a distance, the sign appears to have changed, and I approach it with some curiousness. Sure enough, there is a revised rendition of what this structure shall look like in its completed form. I look at the drawing, then up to this monstrosity, then back to the drawing—and I see that the workers have not yet finished their assembly, for atop the screw-like vertical shaft is now planned a bulbous, asymmetrical head-like thing. I stare at the drawing, which terrifies me with its darkness, with its suggestion of some armless human mutation. I wonder what kind of depraved artist could conceive of such a thing, and I think wistfully of the likes of Raphael, of Botticelli and Renoir.

To the right of the artist's rendition is now a description of this sculpture and, driven more by morbid curiosity than genuine interest, I proceed to read.

> *#dunamisto* is a public art installation financed by a grant from a consortium led by an anonymous corporate donor, the Museum of Contemporary Art, and the Department of Defense. *#dunamisto* is an amalgam of art and technology, a fusion of aesthetics and unprecedented technological advancement. *#dunamisto* represents the anthropomorphization of art and the artification of man, existing in both the abstract form and in reality. *#dunamisto* represents ethical neutrality and takes no position on right or wrong. *#dunamisto* can determine your essence.

I step back from this sign, offended by the text at several levels—not the least of which is its ominous tone. My father was an expert in many disciplines—art and architecture included—and he expressed irritation with those pretentious souls who use the most florid language to describe that which should be accessible to all. He was, for instance, an oenophile and was disgusted by the exclusionary language used by judges of fine wines. "Flabby! Unctuous! Ponderous!" he once railed after reading a particularly highfalutin review of a Cabernet, referring I believe to both the adjectives used by the reviewer and the reviewer himself. My brilliant father's view was that language must be used to facilitate access to complex ideas, rather than to exclude others for the egotistical benefit of those who have already created, mastered and fostered the vernacular of a given discipline. Kingsley Walser—a populist blessed with the most impeccable aesthetic eye— would no doubt have abhorred both this sculpture and the abstruse words used to describe it.

There is also the name of this thing, one that irritates and confounds me. *#dunamisto*. Now, I have not the slightest clue as to why a number sign should precede its name, for there is no number—telephone or otherwise— that follows. What follows this number sign is merely a peculiar name, an unlikely hodgepodge of ancient languages, perhaps, that troubles me. Is it the sculptor's intention, I wonder, to combine roots of both Greek and Italian? To convey a sense of power—a mixed, mutated force? And if so, what does such a name say about this particular work of art? (I am not encouraged.)

And then, of course, there is the reference to a consortium that appears to have provided financial support for this misguided project—some wicked alliance of patrons comprised of the arts, the military, and some unknown business enterprise. And I wonder what these three pillars of our society have to do with each other, why it is incumbent upon them to collaborate on art, to *create* art. Why not leave art to the artist! I say. For all that an artist needs is a flash of inspiration, a pen or a brush, a camera, a stone or a lump of wet clay—and, if divinely blessed, a room with a view. And I say leave commerce to the profiteer—and guns and missiles to the cunning, deathly souls who for centuries have used man's great, imaginative talents to conjure not works of sublime beauty, but instead the trebuchet, the flanged mace, the hydrogen bomb.

And, finally, I wonder what it means to represent *ethical neutrality*, how one could refuse to take even the most tentative position on matters of right and wrong—or how an inanimate object (this sculpture) might have the capacity to make a decision based on ethical consideration, and how and on what basis it might decline to utilize such capacity.

Disturbed, I step further back and gaze up at the sculpture. The two tourists emerge from under the groin of this metal thing and smile as if pleased with what they have experienced. In their socks and sandals, they take a photograph of the structure. They seem to love it—and I shake my head in amazement, for how often have I witnessed a difference of opinion over matters that the rational man sees with the greatest clarity. I can do nothing else but laugh at the illogic of the world, and I shrug my shoulders and move onward. *De gustibus non est disputandum*, as my father often said.

I continue my walk toward Columbus Avenue, where I shall turn right in the direction of the tiny shoe repair shop. I pass the bed store and, in a grand statement, refuse to even look at the shop window—and I take silent satisfaction in the knowledge that the brazen salesman likely notices my protest. After several enjoyable minutes strolling along the boulevard, I come upon this sliver of a shop on Columbus, which is nothing more than a rudimentary shed wedged into the slimmest alley between two buildings.

The shop is at most four feet wide, and I wonder if a broad-shouldered man—a heavyweight boxer or a longshoreman, for instance—could enter without turning sideways. The store's tininess is further magnified by the many things that hang on the interior walls (orthotics, cedar shoe trees, laces and shoe horns) and from the ceiling (purses, totes and potted plants). Immediately upon my entrance I experience a sense of claustrophobia, as if I am trapped, entombed alive. I take an instinctive step back, toward the door, consumed by a fear that this miniscule chamber does not contain enough oxygen to support life.

Behind the counter—which is covered in shoes and parts of shoes—is the proprietor of this establishment, an ancient man with the carriage and tranquil deportment of the most learned wise man. I hold my belt up to him. "Sir, I have come here today with a belt that has little intrinsic value, but carries memories as valuable as a bar of gold bullion." He reaches across the counter with his wise old hands and grabs the belt. "Might you be able to repair it to a serviceable condition?" I ask.

The ancient sage pulls out a magnifying glass and studies the belt. He fingers the two separated flaps and tugs at the partially detached loops. To my great relief, he moans in a manner suggesting a riddle solved.

"Ostrich," he says and holds the belt up to the light. "A *Somali* ostrich."

"A Somali ostrich?"

"Yes ... it is a new species ... it used to be a *sub*-species, but is now distinguished from the common ostrich." I am impressed with, but not surprised by, his knowledge of animal taxonomy. (Is there anything that this man does not know?) The sage tears a ticket from a stack and looks up to me. "Walther?" he asks, with a slight mispronunciation of my name.

My heart leaps with excitement, for I have apparently in past interactions so distinguished myself that this wise man recalls my name. How many nameless, faceless customers have entered and departed this store without having made the slightest impression on him, I do not know—but I am one of the fortunate souls to have left an indelible mark. I am, in some small way, *remarkable*.

"Yes," I exclaim. "It is Walther." I do not correct the spelling or pronunciation of my name, for to do so would insult this wise man.

As I struggle to breathe in this airless vault, he nods and fills out the ticket, tears it in half and, with the steady hands of a watchmaker or a circumciser, passes the receipt to me. "You will need this to claim the belt. Come back in two weeks."

"Of course," I reply. "I shall return in a fortnight." With great deference, I bow to the man as one might bow to a revered swami or pandit or rishi. I quickly exit the suffocating store and, like the man who escapes a burning building, wildly gulp the fresh air. It is at this moment, when I am inhaling and exhaling with obvious fury, that I am approached by none other than Ivan Polsky! As always, the effete snob greets me with a cutting barb.

"Bobby," he says, infuriating me with the use of my diminutive name, "why is it that every time I see you, you appear to be in a state of acute distress? A *sorry* state?" I recall the day when I encountered Polsky and his lady friend outside the papaya and hot dog stand, when I bent down at the waist and reached for my cap after that upsetting interaction with the young girl.

I try to manufacture a cunning retort. "Coincidence," I say.

With a pity that I find insulting, Polsky looks down at me (he is much taller than I thought). He clears his throat and wipes his moist lips with a kerchief that appears from I know not where. He leans close to me, as though he is telling me a great secret. "When there is a pattern of behavior exhibited by one man," he pontificates, "then there is no such thing as coincidence."

My shoulders droop, and I curse this man's impeccable logic. I consider commencing an exercise regimen that will improve my stamina and lung capacity. As he pinches his chin, I recall my father's distaste for this man. "That is a point well taken," I concede, and then curse my limp response.

Polsky smiles with grim satisfaction. He places his hand on my shoulder and exerts some downward pressure, reminding me of both his advantage in height and some perceived supremacy in ranking. "Well, Bobby, it's a real pleasure to see you again." The haughty professor squeezes my shoulder and proceeds uptown, his polished fingernails glistening in the afternoon sun like flecks of mica.

I stand on the sidewalk and look around at the happy pedestrians—men and women, boys and girls—who stroll along the avenue. I remark at the ease with which they seem to enjoy this glorious day, and I wonder if I too shall one day be blessed with such ease. Enervated by my unpleasant encounter with Polsky, I decide to return home and pass the rest of the day with little exertion. I might read a book or prune the bonsai or even take a nap. The thought of an afternoon nap thrills me, for on the rare occasion that I indulge in such a pleasure, I awake from a deep slumber as refreshed and expectant as the swallowtail emerging from its pupa.

At a cocktail party at the Metropolitan Club, I once mentioned my love of the afternoon nap to a self-assured man who identified himself as an investment banker (when he described his job to me, I could not understand what he did for a living). This banker looked at me with skewed eyes, as though I had somehow violated the sacred principles of our professional society. And when I countered that Churchill and President Kennedy were devout believers in the therapeutic effects of the mid-day nap, he took a sip of whiskey and shook his head. "Different era," he said, "there's no time for naps now."

Rather than return home via 72nd Street (at the moment, I cannot bear its commercial pomp), I cross instead on 70th Street—a tree-lined, residential corridor that presents few distractions and even fewer opportunities for inadvertent contact with adversaries such as Polsky or the arrogant bed salesman.

I thus begin my stroll down this quaint side street, passing brownstones on the left and the right; approaching me is a corpulent, bespectacled boy walking a prognathic bulldog (I pity the lengths that this slobbering creature—*the dog*—must go to draw a single breath into its lungs); a Chinese man with a greasy kitchen smock and a cigarette hidden under his palm squats like a baseball catcher and spits into a coffee can (I hear a *plink* when his saliva hits the metal, and I cringe at the thought that this man works in a restaurant); and a butte of over-flowing garbage cans and teeming bags of refuse encroaches onto the sidewalk.

As I near the trash, I quicken my pace out of fear that a rat—a plague-carrying rat—might scamper out from between the bags and run over my feet or bite me on the ankle. (I once had a friend who feared being bitten by horses—and goats, sheep and swine, as well—so it is fair to say that my own fear is not unusual.) What I find interesting about my long-held phobia of rats is that it did not manifest in the presence of sweet Luna, Dame Vivian's hamster. Something about that rodent's domesticated personality and her perfumed coat engendered in me not fear, but the greatest affection. And even though the DNA overlap between hamster and street rat is significant, to me they have as little in common as the silverback gorilla and the harbor porpoise.

I trot past the garbage, keeping an eye on the pavement below. I hold my breath as I pass (the odors can be noxious) and look away from the vile collection. And just as I am about to pass the mound, just as my fear appears to have been unrealized, out from beneath a white plastic bag darts a rat! It is a vile creature with a slick, oily coat, a witch's nose and the claws of a falcon. When it sees me, it freezes for a split second, then boldly scoots across the sidewalk and into the street—where, after rising up on its hind legs, it is swiftly crushed by a truck.

I gasp. I walk over to the edge of the street and look

down at this mutilated animal, which has been flattened like that cartoon coyote after having fallen off a cliff. I look at the rat's fearsome claws and its crushed skull and entrails that slide out of its ruptured body like hot lava. I can identify just one eye, which looks up at me with the deepest regret—at a life cut short, perhaps? At a talent not realized? At a love lost? My thoughts turn to Luna, that delightful creature. I think about the exotic pet doctor and the beautiful mahogany box—and those depraved ruffians who stole Luna's remains. My heart weeps. I am crushed by my failure to protect Luna, by my failure to honor the wishes and the legacy of Dame Vivian Wanamaker. My tender feelings for the deceased centenarian soon turn to recollections of my grandmother, my guardian and loving caretaker after my parents' deaths.

I recall Grandma Sylvia's apartment—the tapestries and tea sets and crystal decanters, the regal Abyssinian cat who luxuriated in a shaft of afternoon light, the portrait of my mother as a young girl (pigtails with royal blue ribbons, a white dress not unlike a wedding gown, an expression of profound sadness). I think about those five years with Grandma—thirteen to eighteen years of age—and her refusal to discuss the deaths of my mother and my father, how we went about our lives as though neither of us had experienced the most devastating loss. "Chin up," she used to say whenever my mood darkened, usually as I lay in bed at night, a book by my side, the transistor radio on so that a distant, soothing voice might keep me company. "Chin up," she would say, turning off the radio and kissing me goodnight.

I again observe the dead rat. From my pocket, I remove a linen kerchief. I bend down and drape the

kerchief over the corpse of this once living thing, this mis-
understood creature that through no fault of its own has
become a global symbol of disease, poverty, and man's
darkest fears. What, I think, has this poor thing done to
deserve such a fate? For is it not deprived of self-will,
lacking the ability to choose its own destiny? If, given the
chance, would it not choose to be something else? (A lilac,
perhaps? Or a bald eagle?) And is not this creature one of
God's many great creations? A gift from God that is equal
in all respects to the silverback gorilla and the harbor porpoise and the Somali ostrich? And why have I projected
my dark fears onto this innocent being, a frightened creature who—like all of us—wants nothing more than a warm
room, nutritious food and a gentle touch?

A tear forms in my eye, so deeply moved am I by the
rat's life and senseless death. I say a prayer for the mis-
understood creature. (It is a Jewish prayer, the Mourner's
Kaddish, which despite my Christian faith has always
moved me with its powerful cadence and rhythm.) "*Oseh
shalom bim'romav, hu ya'aseh shalom, aleinu v'al kol
Yis'ra'eil, v'im'ru, Amen.*"

A man in a tailored suit passes by. He sees me standing in the street, mouthing the prayer, and he stops; he
eyes me with a suspicion often directed at lunatics and
insurance agents. In his attire and arrogance, he reminds
me of the investment banker who disdains naps—and I
find myself outraged by the audacity of these prosperous
few who judge and hold in contempt any behavior that
they believe falls outside of some acceptable band of their
own definition. I stare at him in defiance. "Fuck you," I
mumble and make a peculiar face, one with puckered lips
and flared nostrils. His suspicion confirmed, he turns and

walks away—and I smile, for how the bold woman on the courthouse steps has inspired me.

I resume my walk westward, toward my apartment. So distracted am I by the events of the past several minutes—Polsky and the dead rat, and yet another profane outburst—that I soon find myself at home without any concept of having crossed several avenues and having ascended in the lift to my eleventh floor flat. It is as though I have existed for just a few minutes in some sort of fugue state: active, yet unaware of my activity and the very world around me. I am an observant man by nature, and the concept of walking through life unaware of my surroundings terrifies me—and I am reminded in the most disconcerting way of the oblivious Stavros before his miraculous transformation.

On the mat before my front door is an envelope that is familiar to me, and my breathing deepens in anticipation. I bend down and pick it up, examining the paper, the handwriting, a postmark that indicates a Philadelphia origin—and my heart leaps like a fish on a boat's deck, for I have received a communication from Rose! For the first time since she failed to step off the bus in the Port Authority, my poor, beleaguered Rose has contacted me. I press the envelope against the side of my face and enjoy the sensation of its smoothness. I draw it close to my nose and inhale, and find that—yes—my delightful cherub has sprayed this missive with the most alluring scent, one that I sometimes detect in Sheep Meadow wafting from those guitar-playing girls in their batik dresses. I am delighted, for this is the first time that Rose has offered me sensory evidence of any sort (I have neither seen her photograph nor heard her swallow's voice), and I rejoice at this connection to her. I sniff again, and the name of this scent comes to me. *Patchouli!*

I enter the apartment in an excited state. Before I open the envelope, though, the phone rings. I look at the tiny screen on the handset and see that my agent, Belinda St. Clair, is calling me; she is no doubt furious about my conflict with her loathsome nephew, outraged that I have caused her some embarrassment, and annoyed that I have failed to secure a much-needed income. Fearing Belinda's wrath and eager to read Rose's letter, I allow the call to transfer to the answering machine.

I sit down at the dining room table and place the envelope before me. I tremble, for I know not what traumas will be revealed to me, what woebegone tales, what injustices have been inflicted upon my angel. With a sterling letter opener given to me by my father on my tenth birthday, I open the envelope and remove the card within. Oh how the sight of Rose's elegant cursive moves me. Her perfectly executed letters, her words presented in the straightest lines—all so remarkable in their precision, and even more so in light of her disturbed state. My lips tremble as I mouth the words *Dearest Robert.* I repeat this salutation several times in order to convince myself of its existence. So convinced, I continue—and what I read is a tale that crushes my swollen heart.

My dear Rose reveals that she has endured many trials, including an acute appendicitis that erupted as she waited for the bus that would transport her to me. She describes for me the nausea, the sharp pinch in her abdomen, the sweats that caused her to lose consciousness in the very moments before she was to board the coach. She recounts her futile pleas to the medics. ("Please," she said in desperation, "I *must* get to New York.") My Rose then describes in the most painful detail the intolerable work environment in which she must toil with neither gratitude nor adequate compensation, the venom directed at her by a supervisor who possesses barely a fraction of Rose's intelligence and competence. I am alarmed to learn that she is permitted only a *one-hour lunch*, and my compassion for her thus reaches new heights.

My angel concludes the letter with words of such great affection that I cannot repeat them for fear of diluting their power—but they are words of towering metaphorical force and lofty poetic beauty to which not even the likes of Baudelaire and Rimbaud could aspire. Suffused with the serum of Rose's love, I place the card back in the envelope. I soon find that my earlier fatigue is now magnified by the emotion incited by Rose's letter, and I thus move to the bedroom, to the bed itself, where I run my hand over the inviting sheets. I check my watch and decide that I would indeed benefit greatly from an afternoon nap. I place Rose's letter on the night table and, after disrobing and observing myself in the mirror (I appear more virile than usual), I slip into my pajamas. I turn off the lights and slide under the cool top sheet.

I reach over to the nightstand and turn on the white noise machine, which is set to Rain. The drops of rain, which fall on what I imagine to be a taut canvas tent, hide the ambient street sounds and soothe me. Sometimes I turn the dial to Ocean, Thunder, Summer Night, or Locomotive—but I now miss the sound of rain on a canvas tent. When the first drop of water emanates from the bedside speaker, I recall a distant memory of my father and I spending a night in such a tent, when a thunderstorm pounded our encampment. How safe and cozy I felt knowing that my father, Kingsley Walser—war hero, physicist, minor league baseball player, distinguished professor, and writer—was by my side with a Coleman lantern and a Bowie knife.

As is my pre-sleep custom, I lie on my back and pull a silk mask over my eyes. My arms are folded over my chest like those of an Egyptian king, and I scan my mental library of pleasurable narratives to identify that storyline which will guide me to slumber. I am afflicted with a malady—a common one, I suspect—that prevents me from passing easily into sleep and that instead requires me to imagine the most implausible fantasies, in which I play a leading and often heroic role.

Some nights (or afternoons), the fantasy might involve my playing in the Wimbledon finals against none other than Rod Laver. How I love his versatile game. And in this fantasy, I am nothing more than an amateur—an unknown, unranked amateur who has somehow made his way to the Championships at the All England Lawn Tennis and Croquet Club. The crowd is of course rooting for me, as I am the most unlikely underdog and a symbol of possibility—the possibility that the common man might rise above his predetermined fate and experience success beyond his birthright. (Of course, to do so is impossible.)

We are in the fifth and final set, Rocket and I, and I am ahead by one game: 13-12. That we have played so many games is a testament to our steely nerves, our perseverance, our refusal to surrender. But I have just broken Mr. Laver's serve and, ad in, am now serving for the championship. I notice my opponent leaning slightly to his left, toward the alley. I turn to the stands and wink at the pretty girl in the front row who has been smiling at me since the opening game. A few rows away sit my mother and my father, each adorned with a white straw hat to block the afternoon sun. How proud they look. How they bask in the glory that is their son. I turn back now and prepare for my serve and, still seeing Mr. Laver leaning to his left, I unleash a powerful blast that catches the center line for an ace! The new Wimbledon champion, I throw my racket into the air and run to congratulate the great Australian, who bows in deference to my victory.

I would estimate that I have resorted to this particular fantasy several hundred times in my life, but today, as I lie in my bed with hands clasped over my chest, I cannot bear yet another match with Mr. Laver and instead search for something else to aid in my transition to sleep. I look at the bedside table and see Rose's letter. I reach over and lift it to my nose, inhaling the intoxicating scent of patchouli—a sensory intimacy that has the effect of arousing amorous feelings in me. I return the letter to the side table and, rather than place my hands over my chest, instead slide them under my pajamas, between my legs.

I imagine Rose—her jet black hair; her creamy alabaster skin; her fleshy lips; her body; her breath. A sexual desire overcomes me, and I move my hands accordingly. I picture my own body—the virile version I just witnessed in the mirror—beside hers. I experience a stirring in the groin, a rare and thrilling movement. But before I proceed, a sense of tremendous remorse overwhelms me. "What am I *doing*?" I say aloud. I am consumed with guilt, for the thought of engaging in this fantasy, this intimate act, one undertaken without Rose's knowledge or permission, seems to me improper—as if it is not consensual. I fear that I am defiling Rose, defiling my *image* of Rose. She is a troubled young woman, my dove, and to seek pleasure in her chaste body while she suffers is a sin akin to murder.

I thus withdraw my hands from my pajama pants and cross them over my chest. With the fantasy of Rose now abandoned, I return with reluctance to the Wimbledon finals, but rather than serving for the victory with a 13-12 lead in the fifth set, I am trailing by one game and, down 30-40 on my second serve, facing what is grandly known as championship point. Consistent with my customary fantasy, Mr. Laver leans to his left, toward the alley. But instead of hitting a conservative second serve, a looping kick to his forehand, I blast a hard, flat serve down the center line. "Out!" the linesman screams—and I have lost.

I curse the aggressiveness of my serve, my poor decision-making, my inability to confine my behavior within rational boundaries. I turn to my mother and father, who despite my loss smile with limitless, parental pride. I turn also to the pretty young woman in the front row, who now looks at me not with adoration, but with scorn. She shakes her head in harsh judgment, as if I have failed her—as if I have fallen short of some ideal of her own making.

I consider replaying this fantasy in its customary fashion, such that I emerge victorious. And I consider doing so with the hope of satisfying this young woman—with the hope of making her happy. But I am so tired that I close my eyes and fall into a tortured sleep.

Seven

After ignoring the blinking light of my answering machine for several days, I decide to play the message left by my agent, Belinda St. Clair. I wonder if she is calling about my interview with her repugnant nephew or about my short story that recounts the tale of the brilliant Dutch counterfeiter who cares for his disabled sister. Against my better judgment and at Belinda's insistence (which insistence was prompted by the criticism of the editor of *The Medicine Hat Journal of Short Fiction*), I reluctantly agreed to edit this story so that it came to possess more verve. I started by adding many exclamation points, which created a heightened sense of excitement. (The things that can be done with punctuation!) I then introduced one scene in which the king's truncheon-wielding henchmen chase the counterfeiter through a dark alley and, after much internal debate, I added another scene in which the sister wanders without a clue through a busy street, nearly being hit by several carriages before she is saved by a Jewish contortionist and moneylender.

I press the machine's button as if I am poking a sleeping dog and listen to Belinda's gravelly voice, one formed by years of smoking not just cigarettes, but cigars as well.

"Robert, it's Belinda. A couple things. First, total disaster with my nephew. He thinks you're weird, and I can't say I disagree. I'm not setting you up on any more interviews. You're on your own, sorry. And second, I've got good news about the story. The journal, the one from Alberta, they just called and they're taking it!"

I am annoyed that Belinda has taken her nephew's side, but uplifted by the news of my story, by the fact that the brilliant editor at the journal, a woman of impeccable taste and judgment who resides in a remote Canadian province, has recognized my special talent. I feel great regret at the disparaging comments I made upon my initial rejection, for I now recognize in her an editorial genius that is as rare as the Sumatran rhino or the red-crested tree rat. And while I first bristled at her request for more verve, it was verve—or the lack thereof—that I now admit relegated my story to the heap of unpublished masses. How grateful I am for her editorial guidance, how blessed. And although the consideration paid for such a story is modest, its publication may bring my writing much-needed attention from those omnipotent souls who guard the gates of the publishing industry—those god-like creatures who, from their skyscraping thrones, decide who shall live and who shall die.

Reveling in the glow of my first published work in five years, I decide to take a long walk through the city. I open the window and poke my head out to test the temperature. Sensing a slight chill and the possibility of precipitation, I put on a pair of burgundy corduroys, a button-down shirt, an old hunting jacket, and my father's cap (the very one that the supercilious Polsky pinned to the ground with his precious loafer). Within minutes, I am out on the street and walking toward the park with the confidence of one whose long-overlooked talents have at last been recognized by an expert.

So immersed am I in dreams of my story's impact on the literary world that I pass Stavros's diner with nary a glance in its direction and soon find myself standing within feet of the grotesque sculpture. #dunamisto has changed since my last visit, for atop the inverted Y is now the head of this thing: a twisted, macrocephalic structure that looks down in merciless judgment at the people below. Eyeless, earless, noseless, mouthless (or is that a mouth?), this head nonetheless has a knowing mien—a bulging, knowing mien—that suggests it can see, hear, speak, and smell with superhuman acuity.

I walk over to the sign and again look at the rendition of this thing, and it appears that this beast's design and construction, while not complete, is nearing conclusion. Revised since its prior iteration, the sign now shows a drawing of an enormous screen illuminated with light-emitting diodes—a massive monitor—that is to be installed beside the sculpture. I read the description next to the drawing, but there is no mention of this screen, no mention of its intended purpose. I shrug my shoulders in disgust and continue toward the park, vowing as I go never again to show interest in this dubious work of art.

As I often do, I approach the park near the site of one of our city's most terrible murders. The victim, a musician of note, was a man whom I long appreciated not just for his songwriting talent but for his cosmic misplacement—for he, like me, walked through life as a stranger in a strange land, a kind stranger in an unkind land. I watch as loud-mouthed guides lead herds of tourists—Scandinavians, I think—to the very murder site. I stare as the tourists smile and take photographs, and I wonder why it is that people derive such pleasure from the sacred and the macabre.

I enter the park and walk along a graveled path on which lope two police horses and their uniformed masters. I have great respect for the men, women, and animals of law enforcement, and I bow to them as they pass within feet of me. I resume my walk along this path and notice a cluster of cherry trees in the distance, their rich, pink blossoms swaying in the wind. I find myself mesmerized by these trees, drawn to them as if they were afire and providing warmth on a bitter cold day.

Intrigued, I march in their direction, and my heart races from some distant connection that my mind refuses at this moment to recognize. I walk toward the cherry trees—a small orchard—and notice that one of the trees has been split in half, cleaved by some great force. The tree's dying branches hang down to the ground, leaving a mat of rotting blossoms on the grass below. At the sight of this fallen tree, a powerful emotion from my dark and inner core struggles to actualize, to surge forth and be recognized—an emotion, an *understanding*, that I have suppressed for many years.

The branches of the broken tree have formed a low wooden bench on which I sit. While inhaling the refreshing, cool air, I reach out and pick a pink blossom from a branch. I smell it, and now a tear forms in my right eye.

Whether it is the wind in my face or a painful feeling that is the cause of this tear, I do not know—but I fear it may be the latter. There is a rumbling from within, as if my intestines rage at a spicy food just eaten. But I know that this reaction, this rumbling, has nothing to do with digestion and everything to do with a pain so vast, so potent, and so annihilating that to give it voice may place my very existence at risk.

The rotting branch on which I sit now squeaks—and within seconds, it pops and splits, causing me to fall to the ground. I land with surprising impact and, my head aching from the fall, I lie on my back and look up at the canopy of pink. As if chosen by God, one perfect cherry blossom detaches from a high branch and floats downward like a wounded butterfly, landing with grace on my forehead. When it touches my skin, a current whips through my veins and the sky above appears to turn black. I nod, for I know that my beloved father has spoken to me from the grave.

I think about that day so many years ago, just weeks shy of my thirteenth birthday, when I played the role of Boris Borisovich Simeonov-Pishchik in the school production of Chekhov's *The Cherry Orchard*. Prior to that memorable performance, I was an average boy. I enjoyed comic books and pranks and, although I was a poor athlete, I participated in a multitude of sports. I was a regular boy in the sense that I cared little for my appearance, wearing to my mother's consternation torn jeans and dirty T-shirts, and running to school with my hair in a state of uncombed disarray. In speech, I was prone to the easy vernacular of those times, showing little of my current inclination to formality.

But despite the fact that I was in many respects an ordinary boy, I exhibited tendencies that now seem to define me. I was, for example, afflicted with a propensity to daydream, to withdraw, to misread the social cues that guided others, which caused me to experience a subtle estrangement from my peers. I feared being alone; I feared abandonment; I feared that, other than my parents, no one would ever understand me, love me. Even then, in my early and easy years, there were things about the world that I did not quite understand, and I struggled to connect.

I have often been asked to explain the reason behind my transformation—from what I was to what I am now—and until this very moment I could not identify the cause. But now, as I lie on the ground and stare up at the cherry tree, its pink blossoms painted on the canvas of the blackest sky, its fractured trunk exposing a woody pulp, a thought occurs to me. I recall Act I of *The Cherry Orchard*, when I—as Pishchik—was dressed in the formal attire common to the nineteenth-century Russian aristocrat: a crimson velvet overcoat with an ermine collar, an embroidered silk waistcoat, and high, polished boots.

In this memory, I stand on the wing of the stage and think, *What a silly character he is, this Pishchik.* So steeped in his aristocratic ways while his world collapses around him, while he relies not on his own hard work but good fortune and the generosity of others, all the while charging undeterred toward the abyss of abject poverty. This Pishchik simply cannot let go of the past. And like so many delusional souls, he is afflicted with a tragic flaw that prevents him from accepting the sad reality of his life—the sad reality that the world has changed, but that he has failed to change with it.

So there I stand, stage left, in my aristocratic garb. My beloved father sits somewhere in the audience, although the glare of the stage lights prevents me from seeing him. My fellow classmates are playing the roles of Yermolay Lopakhin, Leonid Gayev, Lyuba Ranevskaya. Poor Madame Ranevskaya! For not only has this regal matriarch lost a young son to drowning, but she has squandered her wealth and now stands through foreclosure to lose her ancestral estate, the beautiful cherry orchard that has been her family's home for generations. (Does nothing lovely *ever* happen in Russia?) And it is when Ranevskaya worries over this great and imminent loss that Pishchik has the audacity to ask Madame for a loan. How self-absorbed of this man, how concerned with his own needs that he fails to appreciate his offense. And when Ranevskaya demurs, citing her own poverty, we see the true and absurd nature of this Pishchik, for he is a man who—like the Stavros of old—walks blissfully through life, but with the irrational conviction that manna of some sort will drop from the heavenly skies and solve his self-inflicted woes. This Pishchik is a man who relies on the good grace of Providence, rather than industriousness, to solve his problems.

Shaken by the anxiety that often comes with public performance, I stand on the stage and deliver my lines with long-rehearsed gusto. "Never surrender. How many times I've fretted, 'I'm finished. I cannot survive.' And then, out of nowhere, someone runs a railroad across my property and they pay me a fortune."

When I conclude my lines and await Madame Ranevskaya's non sequitur of a response ("I have finished my coffee"), there is a commotion in the audience—and

it appears from my vantage point that several theatergo-
ers have risen from their seats. Soon, there is a frantic
shouting that has the effect of halting our production. As
I and the other actors take a few curious steps forward, I
scan the audience and look for my father. But I do not see
him—and my heart aches with a prescience that foretells
catastrophe. The house lights are illuminated, and I can
now see quite clearly what is causing this commotion. In
my aristocratic garb, I leap off the stage and run to my
father—war hero, physicist, minor league baseball player,
distinguished professor, and writer—who lies dead in the
center aisle, his hand clutching his gold pocket watch.
I hurl myself to the ground beside him and weep with
the abandon of the orphaned child. I rest my head on his
chest and listen for the syncopation of his heart—but hear
only a hollow sound that reminds me of a wind passing
through the shell of a conch. And then, I hear *nothing*.

As I lie now in the cherry orchard and stare up at the
canopy of pink and black, my mind and my soul make an
elusive connection—a connection between youth and ma-
turity, between the events that occurred so long ago and
the characteristics that some might say define me now. I
check the time on my pocket watch, my *father's* pocket
watch (which appears to have stopped) and wonder
about the moment he died. I wonder if it is possible for
a human being, a *child*, to experience a trauma so profound that it delivers an irreversible shock to the system,
one that impedes further development and freezes that
person at a specific point in time. I consider my frequent
moments of estrangement, when I feel as if I have been
expelled—like the mutton-chopped carriage driver—from
my proper place in the world and must carry with me the

pain of this dislocation. And I wonder if it was my father's death—while I played the role of this fading Russian aristocrat—that was the cause of my banishment to another century, the cause of my inability to adapt to this modern world. I wonder if it is possible that I, by virtue of the circumstances of my father's death, have been transformed into Pishchik himself.

Eight

꧁

Several days have passed since my revelation in the park, but after much reflection I now harbor some doubt about the connection between an adult identity and the timing and nature of a childhood trauma. I have conducted research at the New York Public Library and have found only a tenuous connection at best, with little basis in the modern psychoanalytic canon to support such a theory. I did, however, stumble upon a 1902 text entitled *Psychopathologia* that was of particular interest, for it presented a case study about a garrulous, professional man from Copenhagen who took his young son on a fishing trip. This man, a financier of some sort, had never before even baited a hook—and as he first cast his line into the sea, his unattended boy fell into the water and drowned. The Danish man experienced such grief that the result was a rapid decompensation, a mental fracture of such epic proportions that he was confined to a sanitarium for six months.

When this once talkative man was released from the mental institution, he spoke little (just a few words per week) and surrendered his career as a financier—and instead spent the rest of his life fishing for salmon in the rivers of Norway. After losing his child while fishing, this man became a *fisherman*. So perhaps, I reason, there is some basis for my theory.

I step out of my apartment on this fine morning and find on my doorstep a brown paper bag. I cannot imagine what might be inside this bag and peer inside with some trepidation. When I angle it so that its dark pocket is brightened by the hall light, I discover that my ostrich belt has been returned to me. I remove the belt and see that it has been repaired with great care, for not only have the loops been reattached with the finest stitching, but the puckered hide now glistens anew as if dipped in a magical polish.

I am perplexed, however, for my recollection is not that I had requested the belt's delivery but that I had agreed to retrieve it from the shop two weeks hence. I am further perplexed by the fact that I have neither provided my address nor paid for the belt's repair, and I wonder how and why the wise old man would deliver the belt to me without proper payment for services rendered. After threading the belt through the loops of my trousers, I decide to visit the cobbler, whom I shall thank for his fine work and compensate for his efforts.

On the way to the tiny shop, I take my customary path down 72nd Street. I pass Stavros, who waves to me amiably with a wide grin and a dusting of confectioners' sugar on the tip of his nose. "Good day," I call out and continue without breaking my stride. I walk with some tranquility past the usual stores—some additive, some diminishing—that have now become so familiar to me that I pay them little attention. These stores are now so woven into the fabric of my daily life that I can no longer recognize them. They have assumed the same status as the sounds emitted from my white noise machine—they are not unlike Rain or Ocean, Thunder, Summer Night, or Locomotive. They exist, but they do not exist.

As I near Broadway, I experience not the contentment of the past several hundred meters, but rather a sense of dread. At first, I am unable to identify the cause of this feeling, this intuition that something dangerous awaits, but when I look up from the pavement, I see none other than *#dunamisto* in the distance—and the cause of my foreboding is instantly explained.

Next to this wretched sculpture (which I had vowed to ignore) now stands a towering screen comprised of the most vibrant and colorful light-emitting diodes. These pinpricks of light flash in an array of ever-changing colors and designs, with no apparent logic or pattern. A worker—the same one who earlier had lowered cables, wires, and switches into the sculpture's bowels—now stands to the side of the screen and works busily on a small computer. He jabs at the keyboard as if he is crushing ants on a picnic table and then looks up to the towering screen. Apparently dissatisfied with what he sees, he shakes his head and returns to inflict even greater abuse on the keyboard. He wipes his sweaty brow with the back of his hand and, after a few seconds of what seems like uneasy contemplation, continues his assault on the keys. He again looks up to see that the lights have stopped their nervous flashing and are now aligned in columns according to color: red, blue, yellow, green, white.

Possessed by a look of the most extreme dismay, he now pounds the keyboard like a frustrated mute who has something important to say. Yet again he directs his gaze to the screen, where a collection of words now bursts forth in brilliant light. I read the words—each of which is familiar to me—but cannot understand the meaning of the sentences created by the sequencing of those words. It is as though the words and their positions have been generated by some random algorithm, resulting in pure gibberish. "Wombat blunt pantaloons dither knave no," reads one line. "Fiend dredge culture sigh native sloth," reads another. At the sight of these nonsensical sentences, the worker howls in lupine fashion. He then raises the keyboard above his head and smashes it to the ground.

The device explodes upon impact and creates a noise so strident that the pedestrians scamper like cockroaches exposed to the light of an opened refrigerator. Stunned by this man's boorish behavior, I, unlike the others, take several steps forward with the intent of chastising him for his inappropriate public display. But as I do so, I notice that he reaches into a toolbox and removes a screwdriver and a mallet. As the man is now armed with tools that can be used as deadly weapons, I quickly recede into the crowd of nervous onlookers.

The worker carries his tools over to the sculpture and uses them to remove a panel at the top of the inverted *V*, just above the beast's open legs. He then reaches deep inside the sculpture and removes a bundle of cables, switches, and wires, does something to them with the tools (God knows what) and then replaces the panel. The worker looks up to the screen, and I follow his gaze.

He smiles in satisfaction, for he has accomplished his assigned task. In a variety of colored letters that gyrate in the most subtle way (like flowers swaying in the soft wind), the screen now projects a complete sentence. "This is a test," it reads.

The crowd, confused just moments earlier, now claps for this man and for this minor technological accomplishment. (How fickle crowds are!) With neither my understanding nor my willing participation, I find that I too am applauding this simple feat, carried along no doubt by the inexplicable power of a crowd. (Why else would a Dutchman offer five thousand gilders and a dozen swine for the bulb of a Viceroy tulip?) The worker, his job completed, picks up the toolbox and broken keyboard and dashes across Broadway to catch an idling crosstown bus.

As if commanded to do so by some higher force, the crowd disperses—some down into the darkness of the subway, some across Broadway, and some, it seems, into the ether. I glance over at the sign that describes this installation and decide to see if it has been amended since my last visit. I find that the artist's rendition has not changed and it thus appears that the sculpture itself is complete, but there is now additional language at the end of the narrative that describes its functionality. (I am confused, for I have always believed that one of art's great attractions is its utter *lack* of functionality.)

"*#dunamisto*," the sign reads, "can tell who you are and why you are who you are. All that *#dunamisto* requires is your physical proximity and a short sampling of your voice."

Alarmed, I turn and look up at the sculpture, at its twisted macro-head, and at the shadow it casts that, like the finger of a ghoul, stretches across Amsterdam and into the papaya and hot dog store. *#dunamisto*'s physical structure alone is enough to trouble me, but the prospect of some foreboding sentience evokes in me a haunting fear—as if the world is on the precipice of madness. I re-read the narrative, looking now for the name of the artist who has conceived of this thing. I again note the financial backing of an anonymous corporate donor, the Museum of Contemporary Art, and the Department of Defense, and my blood boils at the thought of some cynical cooperation among these three institutions, pillars of our great society—commerce, art, and military—that in my view have no business cooperating to produce *anything*, art or otherwise. I wonder about their motives, under what far-fetched scenarios their fundamental principles might align. I continue reading in search of the artist's name but find nothing. And now another thought occurs to me: Is it possible that *#dunamisto* is a sculpture without a sculptor? Have we devolved to a point where art is now being created without the participation of the *artist*?

I am sickened by this possibility and turn my back to the installation with what I hope is finality. With a haste borne of disgust, I stride eastward toward the cobbler's shop, wondering all along about the claim that this sculpture might not only know the truth of a person, but might understand the reasons behind this truth. I think about my own character, about my mother and father, about my tepid writing career and my soul-sickening dislocation. I recall the curious case of the bereaved Dane who fishes for Norwegian salmon. I think about Pishchik. And I wonder if it is possible that *#dunamisto* might discern *my* nature and its elusive causes.

When I reach Columbus, I turn right toward the shoe repair store, which is situated between 69th Street and 70th Street. With my subconscious map and my peripheral vision working in tandem, I stroll down the boulevard and enjoy the sights around me, waiting for my brain to signal my arrival at the shop. I walk for several delightful minutes when I look up at a street sign and see that I am already at 66th Street. Foolish me, I think, I have passed the store. I turn around and walk uptown, this time paying more careful attention to my whereabouts.

As I approach 69th Street, I look forward and to my left, but see nothing and soon find myself again at 70th Street. Perhaps, I reason, my recollection is faulty and the store is in fact farther north—so I continue uptown until I reach 72nd Street, again without any sign of the cobbler's tiny shop. I wonder if I, like the world, am on the precipice of madness—or if I might still be napping and operating within a dream. I pinch the lobe of my ear and experience a pain that refutes the notion of a dream state, which I fear leaves me with a diagnosis of madness. I turn around *again* (how tiresome this has become) and march toward the location where I believe the shop to be, and when I arrive there I discover the reason for my travails: the store has disappeared!

Where the shop once stood, between two buildings, there is now an empty space. A thin alleyway has been created, one that separates the two tenements by just a few feet. I look into the alley for evidence of the shop, for some sign of its prior existence. At first, I see nothing— not even a discarded strip of leather or a shoelace—and I become more sure that some creeping madness is the answer to this riddle. But then I notice that the walls on either side of the alley have two tones of paint. Starting about eight feet from the ground and ten feet from the front of the alley, the walls are a muddy, soot-covered brown, a color and texture that suggests an extended exposure to the elements; but below and before, the walls are lighter in tone, cream-colored, suggesting that these patches have long been protected from the elements and only recently exposed.

I look down and take inventory of what little trash covers the alley floor: a few cigarette butts, a dented beer can, and the front page of a local tabloid. (Oh, dear, they have superimposed a Pinocchio nose onto the face of a once esteemed journalist who was caught in the most unnecessary lie—poor man.) Next to the tabloid, I notice a small, glistening ring, the circumference of which is no greater than that of a sweet pea. I bend down to retrieve this circular piece of metal, and when I raise it to my eyes, I realize that it is an eyelet—the hoop through which a shoelace is threaded.

I walk next door to the corner deli, which as always offers a spectacular array of fresh cut flowers. There, I find the same gentle worker from whom I purchased Rose's tulips—the tiny, Andean man with the flat nose and with the bewildered smile that suggests some confusion as to how he has come to live in this world. He nods to me in a bashful manner and holds up a bouquet of carnations for me to consider. *Carnations*, I think, recalling my mother's distaste for these most proletarian of flowers.

"Thank you, but no thank you," I say, somewhat affronted. "I am not here today to purchase your fine flowers. Rather, I am seeking to understand what has happened to the cobbler's shop."

The Andean appears baffled, as evidenced by the slightest movement of his lower lip. He returns the carnations to a bucket and now holds up for me a bouquet of tiger lilies. "These?" he says.

"No, sir, no," I reply, now frustrated by our miscommunication. "The shoe repair shop? What has happened to it?"

The Andean smiles in the most irresistible way—a pleading smile that begs me to purchase flowers from him, as if such a simple commercial transaction would validate his very existence. "The tiger lilies are lovely," I say, delighted that I shall have fresh cut flowers in my apartment. "I shall take one bunch."

The man smiles and wraps the lilies in white paper. Just as he is about to hand me the flowers, he eyes the carnations. *Please, no*, I think. Sure enough, he removes two of these horrible blue things and inserts them into my bouquet, so that they comingle and miscegenate with my glorious lilies. "For free," he says, proud of his generosity. I am disgusted by their presence, but have not the heart to reveal my feelings to him, for why should a man be punished for the most genuine act of kindness just because the recipient of such kindness is afflicted with idiosyncrasies unknowable to the outside world?

I hand the man ten dollars. "Thank you, kind man, for these beautiful flowers." I hold them close to my nose and inhale, trying to ignore the bitter stench of the carnations.

I turn and look back at the alleyway. I walk several feet until I am standing in front of the dark opening and turn to the Andean. "Sir," I call out. He looks at me, and I point to the space where the wise cobbler's store once stood. I hold the eyelet up for him to see. "What happened?" I ask, pantomiming my inquiry with a shrug of the shoulders and my palms lifted upward.

"Ah! Si, si," he says. He places his hands together, such that the knuckles of each are touching, and then makes a grand, hand-opening gesture that suggests an explosion. "Boom," he says. "All gone."

"All gone?" I mutter, shaken by this strange and terrible news. As if entering some ancient tomb, I step into the alley, into its cool, dark shadows. I extend my arms at shoulder height, and so narrow is the space that I can almost touch both walls with my fingertips. I think about the poise, the serenity, the spiritual strength that is required of a man to work in such a tiny shop for so many years. Gopher-like, I poke my head out from inside the alley and peer at the Andean. "Do you know what has happened to the cobbler?" I ask, with only my head visible to the man. "Is he okay?"

The Andean frowns. With his hand, he makes a cutting gesture across his throat—and then drops his head down to his right shoulder to simulate a death. "Muerto," he says and then returns in the most perfunctory way to the care of his flowers.

I am stunned by the news of this man's demise, for he carried himself with a Buddha-like grace, one that suggested the possibility of immortality. I step out of the alley, into a bright light that seems inappropriate given this sad news, and wonder what has happened to the old sage and his store. Did the shop really explode, as indicated by the florist? I consider the fact that the Andean, given his minimal knowledge of the English language, is a narrator of marginal reliability and may thus have conveyed erroneous information.

I hope it is so, that the flower seller is confused. But if true, *was* there an explosion, one caused by a leak of natural gas? Or by an anarchist? Was the old sage working in the store at the moment of the explosion, and did he die as a result of the conflagration? Or was he absent at that moment, but perished of shock upon hearing the awful news that his beloved shop had been destroyed? (Not likely, as he was far too spiritual a being to develop such an attachment.) Or maybe there was no explosion at all. Perhaps the cobbler passed of causes unrelated to the destruction of the shop—and the landlord then tore it down for some greater (or lesser) use?

Again, like a nervous dog wrapping its leash around a tree, my mind is awhirl with questions unanswered. And further complicating this mystery is the question of the ostrich belt's return to me without payment. I wonder, given the shop's demolition, how and why the wise man delivered the belt to my doorstep? I reach for the belt and admire its puckered hide, its sheen—and I am at this moment affected by an eerie sense of the paranormal, for failed by common experience and science, I am unable to assign a rational explanation to this peculiar set of facts.

It is this thought of the paranormal that reminds me of a childhood event, one that occurred several months after I discovered my mother swinging from the bathroom ceiling. In this memory, my father and I are sitting on the back porch of our rural home in New Hope. We have just finished a gourmet feast cooked by my father: a Lebanese lamb stew, ratatouille, Moroccan couscous, and the most delicious Indian naan. This feast, which was planned to coincide with my mother's birthday, is meant to celebrate both her and her love for those exotic and distant lands she so often visited—but after we finish dessert, I am stricken with a profound sadness, a deep longing for my mother's love that causes me to labor for my breath.

My father lights a cigar, his favorite post-prandial indulgence, and holds the glowing ember up to the dark, moonless sky. He turns to look at me and sees that I am suffering. As he has done so many times before, he places his hand atop my head and musses my hair with an affection intended to soothe me. Just then, as I enjoy the touch of his hand on my scalp, I notice something unusual in the distance—an amorphous, glowing light that hovers ghostly above the nearby swamp.

"What's that?" I ask my father. "That light in the swamp?"

He extinguishes the cigar on the deck's railing and leans forward in his chair. "Well, son, that's a phenomenon called..."

As the light—a greenish, bluish hue—wafts and pulsates in the heat of the summer night, he pauses as if to reconsider his response.

"Actually, I believe it's your mum, Robert," he says with the conviction of a man of great accomplishment. "It's the special way your mum is letting us know she's still here—that she loves us."

"You think?" I say, my lungs clearing, my breath returning to normalcy.

My father wipes his eyes. "I *know*, son."

For many years after that night, especially on the anniversary of my mother's birth, I would look into the darkness in search of those strange, glowing lights, hoping to see some evidence of her pure spirit. But sadly, despite the many hours I stared intently out toward the swamp, I was never again blessed with a visit from her illuminated, spectral form. I often wondered, especially in my youth, why she failed to appear—what great force prevented her from expressing her love from the afterlife. Then there were the bleakest of times when I interpreted the absence of the swamp lights as a sign that my mother—in the great beyond—had again retreated into one of her dark, unreachable moods. And even now, in my adulthood, I often fear that suicide failed to cure her eternal pain.

Years later, when reading a scientific paper on the peat bogs of Scotland, I would come to believe that my father had at first intended to offer an entirely different explanation for those mysterious lights. What I believe he meant to say, before altering his description, was that those ghostly lights hovering above the marsh were what was known as fool's fire, *ignis fatuus*, will-o'-the-wisp—a rare luminescence caused by some combination of gases in the swampy muck. My father possessed a scientific explanation for most complex phenomena, but when he realized that I—his son—required a more inspiring message at that painful moment, he shed his rational ways and instead blessed me with that great gift called *fantasy*. I would also later learn that the actual legend of the will-o'-the-wisp was far darker than the embodiment of my mother's flickering soul, for according to folklore, these misty swamp lights—sometimes the soul of the stillborn, sometimes an evil fairy—seduced travelers with their siren's glow, luring them to deaths most gruesome.

Nine

❦

Today, on the twentieth anniversary of my mother's tragic death, I have received what I can only describe as a glorious gift, one that comes directly from the hands of a benevolent and loving god. My dear Rose, my precious angel, has sent me a letter in which she has included the most unexpected surprise: a photograph of herself. I press this image close to my heart, for how beautiful she is. Far more beautiful than I could have ever imagined, and not dissimilar from the mental image that I had drawn of her. As I had anticipated, her hair is dark black and smooth, and cut just above her majestic shoulders; her skin is the palest white, unblemished except for an intoxicating mole to the right of her nose; her lips are more pale and thin than I had imagined, but enticing nonetheless; and her smile is crooked and tense in a way that suggests a weariness of the soul.

But what surprises me most about her appearance is her attire, for she (like me) appears to come from a different era. My angel wears a pink petticoat, full and frilly, a white blouse that is loose in the sleeve and, above her blouse, a tight red corset from which hang loops of embroidered, gold silk. Lace tea gloves—ending just below the second knuckle—adorn her hands, and on her feet are high, black boots that remind me of something Boris Borisovich Simeonov-Pishchik might wear. Her aesthetic suggests to me something from the nineteenth century, although I cannot identify the geography to which her attire is indigenous. My Rose, I conclude, is an unusual combination of the Wild West and Victorian England.

Accompanying her wardrobe, though, are strange, futuristic accessories that imply some space-age modernism but at the same time harken back to centuries past. In her right hand, she holds a steel weapon that resembles a Buck Rogers ray gun, and on her right shoulder is a brass epaulette on which is welded a pneumatic pump of some sort. I have never before seen such an ensemble and am thus perplexed. I turn to the photograph's back, on which Rose has in her smooth cursive written the words *Me at the steampunk cotillion*.

I wonder what she means by this word *steampunk*, for it is unfamiliar to me. Intrigued, I open my Oxford English Dictionary and search for the word, but I find nothing in between *steamie* and *steamroller*. (Also unfamiliar to me is this word *steamie*, which I now learn is a public washing area and often a venue for gossip—and I wonder how I can incorporate this puckish word into my story about the brilliant Dutch counterfeiter who cares for his disabled sister.)

My dear Rose has further blessed me with an invitation for which I have long awaited: it is a request for me to visit her in the city of Philadelphia just one week hence! After so many months of a relationship based entirely on correspondence, I shall at last be united with my love—my gorgeous, steampunk angel—and be able to hold her quivering body in my reassuring arms. And not only has Rose extended to me this invitation, but she also has offered to pay for my bus fare. Several weeks ago, in a moment of shameful weakness that I now regret, I disclosed to her the full nature and extent of my financial challenges—and she is thus willing to use her few remaining dollars to purchase for me a train ticket.

Like Saint Teresa of Calcutta, Rose is the type of woman—one in many millions—who eagerly abstains for the benefit of those less fortunate. But despite her generosity and my own predicament, I shall not accept her gift, for to do so would violate a sacred social compact—one that was taught to me by my father. "Robert," he said to me just days before his death, "under no circumstances should you ever accept money from a woman, no matter her wealth or your lack thereof, for it is better that you buy her the simplest meal than to accept from her a six-course feast. Wiser to live a modest life, the life of a monk, than to disrupt that delicate balance between man and woman. And beware the common trap—the illusion that your love for each other is so great that the balance cannot be disrupted." So, in honor of my father and this delicate balance, I resolve to make my way to the Cradle of Liberty with Rose's subsidy respectfully declined.

So elated am I by the contents of this letter that I decide to go have a shave, for is there a greater treat than a grooming by the hands of a professional? Just around the corner from Stavros's place is an old barber, a Turk from the island of Cyprus whose disgust for the diner owner is so great that he refuses to eat the Greek's fine pastries. In fact, he holds Stavros in such contempt that with shameless mischief he has often invited Stavros in for a shave, an offer that the Greek has long ignored for fear of being slashed in the barber's chair.

I believe that Stavros's fear is legitimate, as the Turk fumes incessantly about some Cypriot village overrun by rapacious Greeks—and in his pocket he carries a photograph of his ancestral home that he vows one day to retake from a family of Athenians known as Fotopulos. "If I have only one breath left," he will start as he lathers my face and throat—and from there he will go on and on about the Ottoman Empire and the superiority of Turkish food and the dangers of the Greek unification movement he calls *enosis*, all the while shaving me with the precision of a diamond cutter.

I enter the barbershop and am disappointed to see that the Turk's chair is occupied by a customer, one whose face is covered with hot towels. The two men are engaged in an animated banter, laughing with the familiarity of old friends. I watch how the Turk draws the blade of a straight razor across the customer's thick neck, how he admires the closeness of the shave and wipes the mixture of cream and stubble on a towel. As the barber tends to the flesh below him, the two men discuss the current state of a particular New York baseball team that continues to torment its beleaguered fans with inept play. And when the man in the chair mumbles through the hot towels that the team's shortstop cannot hit a volleyball, the Turk sighs with an exasperation that suggests he has long suffered over the plight of this particular team from Queens.

As if he has just noticed that I have entered the shop and am standing no more than three feet away, the Turk looks up at me with surprise. "Five minutes," he says, somewhat irritated by my presence. "Just need to finish shave."

I take a seat on a low bench and flip through the selection of magazines. I am interested in neither *Cyprus Monthly* nor the tawdry collections of gossip and celebrity scandal. Instead, I admire the Turk's mastery of his craft and wait patiently for him to finish the shave. After scraping the final dollop of cream from the customer's neck, he rubs an aloe balm on the irritated skin. He then lifts the hot towels from the man's face—and I rub my eyes as if I have just seen an extraterrestrial, for who should be reclining in the chair but *Stavros*!

I wonder how it is possible that these two men—the bitterest ethnic enemies—have become so friendly. What has happened to the enmity that for so long caused the Turk to refuse the Greek's chocolate bear claws? Is it conceivable, I wonder, that Stavros has experienced a psychic transformation so dramatic that he can not only embrace a love between homosexuals, between lesbians, but that he can also heal the wounds of an ancient feud? Is it possible that Stavros, of all people, has become a *god among men*?

Stavros, who appears to be cured permanently of the incomprehensible idiocy of old, rises from the chair and admires his clean-shaven face in the mirror. Other than the perfectly trimmed moustache, how smooth and shiny his skin looks. When he turns to leave, he notices that I am standing before him. "Walser!" he exclaims, as if we have encountered each other by chance in the most remote and distant port. "How you feeling? All recovered from that nasty flu? Kilkenny told me you were sick as a dog."

I recall the impertinent doctor and his ludicrous suggestion that I suffered not from a virus or bacterium, but from a psychosomatic illness of some sort. "Yes, thank you. I have fully recovered."

Stavros bids me adieu with the promise of a free cruller, and I settle into the Turk's cushioned chair. The barber leans the chair back so that I am reclining. He massages my scalp with the tenderness of an adoring lover, then drapes hot towels over my face and neck. I am encased in darkness and in a relaxing, moist heat—and within moments I am fast asleep, in a slumber so deep that I have no concept of the passage of time. After a pleasurable dream involving Rose (we are in a rowboat with a puppy), I am awakened by a tap to the crown of my head, and when I lift my heavy eyelids and look into the mirror, I am delighted by the adolescent glow of my skin—and can only imagine the favorable reaction that dear Rose will have to my radiant complexion.

After paying the Turk and asking him why a baseball player would be asked to hit a volleyball (he appears even more irritated than before), I step out onto the sidewalk. I consider the route of my walk, where I should stroll on this resplendent day. Rather than walking west to the dreadful river (with its whitecaps that remind me of the sharp teeth of a rabid fox), I decide to return to the park, to the cherry orchard that so captivated me. There, I shall revisit my theory about being frozen in time as a result of some great trauma—and I shall imagine how Pishchik might live in the New York of today. And despite my distaste for the grotesque sculpture outside the subway station, I resolve to visit that atrocity on the way to the park, to gauge its development and to see about the purpose of its giant screen.

My freshly shaven skin tingling in the rays of the morning light, I arrive several minutes later at the intersection of 72nd Street and Broadway. A palpable energy fills the plaza—for there, in all its artistic-military-industrial glory, stands the towering *#dunamisto*. I am surprised to see that a long line of the admiring and the curious has formed in the plaza, waiting, it seems, to enjoy this work of art, to test the functionality of this thing—to determine if indeed *#dunamisto* "can tell who you are and why you are who you are."

At the front of the line is a man who, like so many others in the city of late, appears to be a Scandinavian tourist. (Is it conceivable that every citizen of Norway, Sweden, and Finland has been expelled from their home country at the same time?) A uniformed man stands beside the sculpture, and whether he is a police officer, private security, or military, I do not know. From my vantage point across the plaza, he appears to be humorless and precise in his movements, detached emotionally from the world around him. Perhaps these traits—which are ineffective in most other contexts—are requirements for this particular job. The man waves to the tourist and signals for him to step forward, to stand under the legs of the inverted *Y*. The tourist, possibly a Finn, complies and walks under *#dunamisto*'s spread legs. From his subordinated perspective, this possible Finn looks up to the behemoth's imposing, steel groin and, somewhat embarrassed, says "I am Björn from Uppsala, Sweden... and I work in the insurance industry."

The crowd chuckles for reasons unclear to me (perhaps because he sells insurance). There is a moment of anticipation during which I wonder what is happening inside this structure, what type of techno-psychological analysis, if any, those wires and cables within are conducting. I am curious to see how this *#dunamisto* reacts to the Swede's minimal disclosure. Prompted by the uniformed guard, the man peeks out from the darkness and looks up to the massive screen, his gaze followed by those in line and by many in the gathering crowd, myself included. Soon there is a flashing of colorful lights on the screen, rapid bursts that closely mimic the fireworks one might see on the Fourth of July: the Roman candle, the falling leaf, the peony, the strobe. How glorious these lights are! And how beautifully choreographed are their explosions. And with each burst of these electronic lights, the crowd gasps as if actual pyrotechnic explosions boom in the sky above, painting our faces with flashes of red, white, and blue.

The screen goes dark, and there is an audible gasp from the audience. In my experience, this audible gasp is a customary response, representing the disappointment of a fireworks show ended, coupled with the hope that the grand finale is yet to come. A few seconds pass and a word begins to form on the screen, one letter at a time— as if it is being typed by some invisible hand. This first word—*Björn*—is followed by more words, which are created with greater speed, as though the creator of this text is becoming more adept at this form of communication. (I am quite impressed that *#dunamisto* has included the umlaut.)

"Björn Svenson," the screen reads, somehow noting the man's last name, "is the son of a fisherman and the first member of his family to attend university." I watch as the Swede smiles uncomfortably in agreement. "Björn Svenson," the thing continues, "is a committed professional with a deep understanding of actuarial tables and the pricing of risk, although he lacks the interpersonal skills necessary for maximum career advancement. For three years, he has been involved in a romantic relationship with a woman named Elsa, a graduate student in psychology, yet he is ambivalent about the institution of marriage."

The Swede opens his mouth to express shock at the sculpture's insight, then shrugs his shoulders sheepishly, eliciting a laugh from the crowd.

"He is prone to bouts of melancholy, especially during the winter months, and longs to relocate to a warmer climate. He is unable to relocate, though, because he is committed to supporting his elderly parents during the final years of their lives. Fearful of conflict, Björn Svenson is left-handed and wears contact lenses. He enjoys tennis and jigsaw puzzles."

The Swede places his hand to his chest, a gesture designed to convey great shock. *Yes, yes,* he nods to the crowd, indicating that *#dunamisto* has been accurate in its analysis. I however am unimpressed, for there is no doubt that what I have just witnessed is nothing more than a cheap carnival act—one in which this "tourist" is in actuality a paid participant in a childish stunt. I assume that my rejection of this charade, of this glorified fortune-teller, is shared by the onlookers, but I am shocked to see that they instead react to these computer-generated words with marvel, as if they have just witnessed a shackled Houdini escape from an underwater tomb.

At this moment, my affection for the masses is replaced with pity, for how foolish must one be to believe that this inanimate object has just described a complete stranger with such accurate detail? How can these lambs be so innocent, so trusting? (Especially in light of the disturbing combination of sponsors who have provided the grant for this gloomy sculpture.) As the screen fades to black, the Swede exits the monster and joins several sandal-clad friends who congratulate him for I know not what. (For a role well acted?)

Next in line is a middle-aged woman of considerable girth. The uniformed man beckons her to enter the space between *#dunamisto*'s legs, and she proceeds with great caution, as if she fears that she might not fit into the triangle-shaped opening at the base of the sculpture. But given the enormity of this thing, she inserts herself into the space without any trouble—and when the man gives her an affirmative hand gesture, an indication to proceed, she looks upward and says, "My name is Helen and I live in central Iowa. My husband is a retired long-haul trucker and my grand-aunt was an army nurse."

She smiles coyly at the crowd, and I believe that she does so because she is convinced that she has stumped this miscreation with her vague brevity. Again, the enormous screen blinks pyrotechnically and spews forth a blizzard of fireworks before turning dark and publishing its analysis of this Iowan.

"Helen Schweitzer suffers from a deep insecurity brought about by her inability to lose weight. Although she maintains that she has a problem with her metabolism brought upon by hypothyroidism, the truth is that she is sedentary and eats too many sweets and fatty foods. Helen Schweitzer has been married to the same man for thirty-five years, and although she sometimes flirts with the night manager at the local market, she has been faithful to her husband. She is right-handed, has 20/40 vision, and engages in sexual intercourse infrequently. She enjoys scrapbooking and gardening."

This woman, unlike the Swede, appears disturbed by *#dunamisto*'s analysis—as evidenced by a torrent of tears and a hyperventilation that borders on histrionic. She storms out of the sculpture and, covering her face with her purse like a criminal trying to avoid the press, pushes through the crowd. Without even looking to see if she has the right of way (she does not), this Helen Schweitzer waddles across Broadway—where she is almost hit by a cab—and continues west toward the dreadful river. The crowd looks on in horror, but I—an astute man—am again unpersuaded, for I know that what I have just witnessed is nothing but a cunning ploy by these charlatans—whoever they might be—to insert some realism into this most implausible scenario. And as I watch the alleged Iowan disappear into the chaos of a city street, I wonder which renowned acting school this talented performer has attended.

I look up at *#dunamisto*'s mutated, twisted head, which stares down at me with supercilious condescension. I am at first intimidated and look away, but then quickly gather the fortitude to glare defiantly back at its malformed dome, to reestablish the dominance of man over machine. (Sadly, I fear, we have not seen the last of each other.) Disgusted by *#dunamisto*'s cynical manipulation, I proceed in the direction of the park and on my way approach the iconic shop that sells hot dogs and papaya juice. For once, there is no line extending out to the sidewalk, and what arises in me without warning is some long suppressed desire to sample this sweet-and-savory fare. I look around to see if any critical souls lurk nearby. (Is that Polsky? Wearing a beret atop his head? No, no, it is just another effete snob.) Satisfied that I am unobserved, I enter the store.

Upon my entry, I am met with the most tantalizing aromas of cooked beef, brine, and tropical fruit. The man behind the counter asks for my order, but before proceeding there is one question I feel compelled to ask. "The fruit juice, sir? The papaya? Is it fresh squeezed or made from concentrate?" With a curl of the lower lip, the man appears as irritated as the Turkish barber, and I wonder what it is about the Upper West Side today—why the whole neighborhood seems to be in the foulest of moods.

The man looks right and left. "You see anyone squeezing fruit here?" he asks.

I look around the small area. "No, sir, I do not."

"Well, there's your answer," he growls. "Your order?"

I order one hot dog and one small cup of papaya juice from concentrate and, after paying the most trifling sum, step out to the sidewalk. I again look around for the presence of a familiar face and am relieved to see only strangers. After inhaling the smoky scent of the hot dog, I take a sip of this famed papaya juice—and how delicious it is. So sweet and smooth, so aromatic! I believe that it is not only tasty, but that it possesses significant health benefits, as it is rich in vitamins A and C, induces a healthy glow in the skin, and, I once read, even regulates menstruation (in women). I now bite into the hotdog, my teeth puncturing the leathery casing before sinking into the tender meat within. Briny water explodes from the delectable wiener and drips down my chin, and I find myself in the most unlikely culinary heaven. Having partaken of these treats, I now understand the allure of this combination of savory and sweet, and this shop's rightful place in our zeitgeist. And so delicious is this meal that I quickly devour the frankfurter and, sucking hard on the straw, drain the juice from the cup.

After disposing of my trash in the wastebasket, I walk east toward the park—toward the cherry orchard and its great mysteries. The sky is alive with puffs of cotton that move as if propelled by a gale; birds dance a tarantella atop the light pole; and a trumpeter plays "Freddie Freeloader" on the sidewalk. As I stroll along, my soul is infused with the vitality of this great city and its myriad surprises.

But when I am just meters shy of Columbus Avenue, my mood changes, for I experience a rumbling in the gut—a growl reminiscent of that of an angry cur. This growl is followed by a sharp pain in the abdomen, as if I have been pinched with great force. My brow sweats and my cheeks flush—and it is apparent to me that I am suffering from some adverse reaction to the food and beverage I have just consumed. I now regret my silly foray into that unsanitary place, for how disgusting that shop is! With its vile tubes of salty meat! With its sugary juice and its haughty counter boys! How this shop has become an iconic establishment in this city is beyond my comprehension and is the saddest reflection of the state of our mindless society, one that is obsessed with salt and sugar (and other assorted pornographies).

Overcome by the fear that I may soon defecate in my pants, I shuffle back toward my apartment in short, choppy steps. On the way, I pass the vulgar mattress salesman, who stands in front of his store and waves a flyer of some sort. "Hey you," he yells. "Wanna buy a bed?"

I pause and bend over at the waist. I look up at him and consider the corrosive effect that he and his store have on society. "Never," I groan—and with the flick of his wrist, he offers me his promotional materials.

Flyer in hand (they are offering a 30 percent discount!), I continue my agonizing shuffle west, past the site of my poisoning, then past *#dunamisto* and the teeming crowd of admirers. I glance up to the screen to see that a digital pyrotechnic show is in full bloom. I am curious to see the words that come next, but am in too much agony to wait. With each short step, the pain builds and takes me even closer to that sad, public humiliation known as incontinence. I soon see my apartment building in the distance, and something about the proximity to my home sends a signal to my bowels that we are near—and my ability to restrain myself is thus even more severely compromised.

Fearing that at any moment I may lose control of my bowels, I bend over and look around to see who might bear witness. And, of course, whom do I see approaching? It is none other than the imperious Polsky! I marvel at this man's ability to appear at my moments of greatest distress, and I quicken my pace to elude him. I turn into my building before he can greet me, but as I slip into the lobby and close the door, I hear his affected voice call out to me. "Bobby! *Sorry*, Bobby!"

"*Sorry*," I growl. I squeeze my legs together and press the elevator button—and am met with evidence of the existence of some divine creator, for the lift's doors open immediately and I am carried upward with the speed of a rocket. Within seconds, I am safely positioned on my toilet seat, my fear of public humiliation abated. And with my anxiety so lessened, I find that my physical pain too has diminished substantially. My thoughts turn to the quack Kilkenny and his speculative diagnosis of a psychosomatic ailment, and I consider the possible connection between mind and body—if there might indeed be a causal link greater than which I had long thought possible.

Within an hour, my system purged of all toxins, I lie on the couch tired but in relative comfort. I look around my chamber and observe the mementos of earlier times, of *better* times: my father's cap, which hangs from a hook on the wall; framed in glass, the ticket stub from the baseball game he took me to as a child; a pair of Dutch clogs painted with tulips, the klompen dancing clogs; the portrait of my mother as a young girl (pigtails with royal blue ribbons, a white dress not unlike a wedding gown, an expression of profound sadness). A familiar melancholy gathers strength within me, and as I am uncomfortable with such a feeling, I try to divert my mind's attention from the evidence of my great loss.

I look over to the answering machine on the desk and notice that its amber light blinks. Relieved by this distraction, I rise and press the button, which reveals a message from my agent, Belinda St. Clair. I listen to her tar-scarred voice and am devastated by her message, for it seems that I have suffered yet another unexpected disappointment.

Belinda informs me that the editor and sole proprietor of *The Medicine Hat Journal of Short Fiction* has died (my agent does not know the cause, although she suspects methamphetamines) and that the journal has been forced to file for protection under Canadian bankruptcy laws. She goes into extraordinary detail about the financial predicament of this journal—so much detail that the machine, apparently exhausted by her verbosity, terminates the call mid-sentence. Undeterred, Belinda calls back and leaves another message, this one describing a further complication that she claims could not have been anticipated.

"You signed a contract with the journal giving them the right to publish the story—*exclusive* right. In exchange for three hundred dollars, remember? And because it's in bankruptcy court now, you're stuck. Your story's now part of the estate—creditors and all that. So you can't get it back until we get the contract voided, recover the rights. We'll be fine, but it'll take some time."

I walk to the kitchen and, upset, pour myself a half glass of Chablis. I sit down at the dining room table and ponder the implication of this news. I have written a fine story, one with verve; this spirited story was accepted for publication by a journal that, given the hard work and intelligence that were required to create such a smart story, paid me a mere pittance; this same journal and I executed a contract governing the use of and payment for said story; I have not received a penny of the agreed-upon fee; the journal has, without warning, ceased its operations; and I am somehow not permitted to publish elsewhere until such time as a bankruptcy trustee decides to liberate my story. Is it possible, I wonder, that a writer, an artist, can be legally stripped of the rights to his own work? Is that possible? Is it conceivable that such a thing can happen in a modern democracy at this moment in time?

This distressing news activates in me the fear of financial ruin. (How could it not?) For many years now, I have sought gainful employment, only to be turned away by petty tyrants for, I presume, the transgression of my supposed non-conformity. Why, I ask myself after each rejection, must the workforce be limited to those who adhere to the social norms of our day? Is there not room, too, for a man with a fin-de-siècle sensibility? A man who is unencumbered by the existential angst of this nuclear age? With a different and refreshing perspective to offer? Sadly, it seems not.

I lift myself from the seat and retrieve my bank statements and bills. Given my facility for most things arithmetical, I am able to establish with ease that I have funds adequate to last me only another three months—after which point, and absent meaningful income prior thereto, I shall incur a crippling deficit. It is this dire prospect that prompts an irksome recollection of the excessively compensated creative director—my agent's nephew—and causes me to curse a society in which an arrogant man, one who glorifies drug-addled murderers like Sid Vicious, is fêted as if he were the second coming of Henry Ford.

So drained am I by my bout with financial insecurity and with parasites or protozoa—or whatever microorganisms have infected me—that I repair to my bedroom, disrobe, and slide under the sheets of my bed. I place the silk mask over my eyes and am so exhausted that I find myself drifting off with haste. But just as I have reached that hazy transition between consciousness and sleep, when bizarre images mix with reality to form a surrealist stew, my heart races with the recollection of Rose's steampunk photograph. I lift the mask from my face and retrieve the picture from my side table. There she is, my angel, in her pink petticoat, full and frilly, her white blouse that is loose in the sleeve, her tight red corset from which hang loops of embroidered gold silk, her lace tea gloves. I draw the photograph closer and examine her Buck Rogers laser gun and the pneumatic pump that sits atop her shoulder. Oh what a sense of humor my Rose has—and how I adore her cheeky combination of past and future.

At the sight of Rose in her steampunk attire, I find myself aroused—a not uncommon reaction when I am in bed and my thoughts turn to her. I place my right hand beneath my undergarment and commence a motion that further enhances my pleasure. I imagine her removing her corset, her blouse, her petticoat—her *laser gun*. But, mere moments from culmination, I am again afflicted with guilt, troubled that I am engaging in a sordid, non-consensual act that defiles her purity. (Why must I turn my innocent angel into a strumpet?) Ashamed of my base instincts, I remove my hand. I reposition the eye mask and commit to slumber. As I lie on my back, however, my arms crossed over my chest, I realize that my tumescence has not subsided. I curse myself and my physiological wiring, for I am no better than the untamed beast on the savannah.

Enticed by my rigidity, I return my hand to its position between my legs, where I resume a titillating motion. As I continue this movement, I become aware that the guilt of my unilateralism has disappeared and has been replaced by a reciprocal eroticism, a sense that I am providing my love with the physical intimacy that she so craves, and that she provides me with the same. I imagine my saucy Rose removing the garter belt from her right thigh, how she snaps it like a rubber band, and how it hits me in the chest—*how we laugh!* It is in this fantasy of partnership that Rose comes to me, embraces me, devours and loves me for the antiquated man that I am; it is in this fantasy that I no longer fear exploiting her for my rank sexual gratification, but instead revel in the pleasure that I bring her; it is in this fantasy that we come together as the most tender lovers. And with these thoughts in mind, I now imagine my imminent trip to Philadelphia and the romantic pleasures that we will, in actuality, bring each other.

I continue with the movement of my hand until I reach the acme of my desire, a discharge pearly and luminous, and a burst of the hormone oxytocin that only magnifies my great love for the enchanting Rose. I experience a state of the most sublime euphoria, as if I have inhaled a potent opiate. I draw the mask over my eyes, ridding myself of any visual evidence of a world that might exist outside the boundaries of my own mind.

"Good night, my love," I whisper. "Next week in Philadelphia."

Ten

I awake this morning in the foulest mood—furious with the papaya and hot dog shop, for how they harmed me with their repellant and unsanitary fare. With the moral authority of the Methodist minister or the ferry-boat captain, I march out of my building and toward the contemptible shop, where I plan to seek both financial restitution and an apology. So enraged am I that I am at first oblivious to my surroundings and pass the familiar stores and landmarks with the speed of a quarter horse. (Out of my peripheral vision, I believe I see Stavros holding a pecan strudel up for me to see, but I do not stop.) I quickly reach the chaotic intersection at Broadway and look across the junction at the offending shop. As usual, a long queue has formed on the sidewalk. I wonder if a man seeking restitution and an apology must wait in line with those who seek to purchase this nasty grub, or if such a man may cut to the front of the line and air his grievances without having to suffer the further indignity of delay. I believe that he has the moral authority to do so, but I fear that a hungry customer might not recognize this authority and would thus react with aggression.

As I am poised to cross the avenue and assume my place at the end of the line, I see *#dunamisto* standing above me. I am startled, for so immersed was I in retribution, so focused on confronting those purveyors of putridity, that I looked past this mutated horror disguised as art. But now that it has caught my attention, I find that I cannot take my eyes off of it. Something about the sculpture has changed—or maybe it is my perception of the thing that has changed.

Where the sculpture once terrified me with its mass of dark steel and with the long shadows it cast over humanity, I now see a gentler, softer version of this foreboding monster. The head, once gnarled and twisted in some expression of terror, seems to have unwound and now projects a countenance of kindness, of hospitality. The open triangle formed by its legs, which intimated at some sort of abnormal reproduction, is now flooded with the light of the reborn. Even the thing's cold, industrial skin now welcomes, with flecks of mother-of-pearl dancing in the light. So astonished am I by this transformation that my feelings of ill will, while not eliminated, recede—and I wonder if the worker who programmed the screen has also given *#dunamisto* a conscience, a soul.

I walk over to the sign to see if there is an explanation for this metamorphosis—one that in magnitude and surprise rivals the transformation of Stavros. I read, but see that there is no reference to the sculpture's altered appearance. I look back at *#dunamisto* to confirm that the structure has indeed changed (it has) and, confused, I return to the sign. The only addition since my last reading is what is described as a Privacy Policy (written, of course, in tiny font at the bottom of the sign).

This Privacy Policy reads as follows:

> When you enjoy *#dunamisto*, we collect a variety of information. This information may include your physical characteristics, such as your hair color and texture, eye color, skin color and tone, fingerprints, weight, and height. This information may also include personal details that you disclose to *#dunamisto*, such as your name, hometown, occupation, and any other information you share with us. In addition, when you enjoy our installation, we may undertake certain analyses of you and your character. These analyses, which are based in part on the information that we collect and that you provide, are developed through the use of *#dunamisto*'s proprietary technology and may be used by us and our financial sponsors for any reason.

Troubled by the wording of this policy, I step back from the sign. I resent its breezy familiarity, its manipulative use of the second-person point of view, which suggests that we are somehow acquainted. My belief is that a legal disclaimer should sound like a legal disclaimer—with words such as *hereof*, *thereto*, and *hereunder*; a legal disclaimer should not, I maintain, sound like a letter between friends. I wonder what the consortium of patrons—this odd trio comprised of commerce, art, and military—might do with our information, what purpose these analyses of our characters might serve, what value they might have. And, of course, I worry about the phrase *for any reason,* for such words are without limit and create the greatest opportunity for abuse.

I turn and look up at *#dunamisto,* which continues to dazzle me with its newfound appeal. Not far from the sculpture sit several teenagers, one of whom uses a phone to take a digital photograph of the others. She examines the captured image and, pleased, presses what I assume is a button on the glass screen. "Just posted it," she says to her friends. She then extends her right arm and takes a photograph of *herself,* with *#dunamisto* looming over her shoulder. Again, she presses the screen. "That one too," she confirms. I wonder what it is about this generation, how they show no concern for the protection of their own privacy, how they freely share with the world— with anonymous strangers—every kiss, every meal, every failure and petty victory. I wonder what has happened to those lofty, bygone principles known as discretion and modesty.

These thoughts of privacy trigger a recollection of a novel that I once read by a Czech writer, a modernist. (I did not understand this novel, as there was so much infidelity that I could not keep track of who was having sexual intercourse with whom. I also do not understand modernism.) Anyway, this Czech writer described the loss of privacy and free expression following the Soviet invasion of his beloved country in 1968—how an oppressive state apparatus denied individuals the right to keep even their most intimate secrets, and how the brave citizens of Prague went to the most ingenious lengths to hide even the most immaterial facts of their lives.

I think now about our own society, and an idea forms. Perhaps these children who use their telephones and computers to share everything with the world are not the vapid fools so decried by the older generations, but rather the most brilliant and daring rebels. For maybe these adolescents understand that to wage war against the omnipotent forces—whose very *raison d'être* is the acquisition and use of our most private information—is futile. Perhaps they realize that in *their* world, there can be no Velvet Revolution, no generational shift to free them from the grip of this data tyranny. They understand what the rest of us do not: that we are doomed to an irreversible imbalance of power. And as they accept the reality that the ownership of information is beyond their influence or control, they fight by *not* fighting—the most subtle form of passive resistance. They, I submit, may be wiser than the rest of us.

I consider the possibility that this generation may not be as narcissistic as we adults might think; it may in fact be that what they are really doing by exposing themselves to the world is something akin to a country's printing too much money. They, like my Dutch counterfeiter, are devaluing a currency—in this case a currency called data. "If you want to know five things about me," they say without so saying, "then I shall give you fifty thousand. And do with it what you damn well please, for I do not care. We will flood the market with so much data that it will be worthless."

By publishing without filter the minutiae of their lives, I suspect that this generation is in actuality yelling the heartiest objection. And all the while enjoying themselves. Good for them! I say. Good for them!

I move closer to *#dunamisto* and watch as an elderly man steps out from the legs of the sculpture. He and the crowd look up to the giant screen, which explodes in pyrotechnic glory. I wait for the analysis that will soon follow, for the cutting critique that will be published for all to see and that will leave this sweet old man in a state of humiliation and distress. The fireworks conclude—and within seconds, words begin to form on the screen.

"Edward Bristol of North Caldwell, New Jersey, is a kind man, modest and reliable, who is adored and respected by all who have had the privilege of knowing him."

I watch as a wide smile consumes the face of this Edward Bristol. A thunderous crack of applause rises from the delighted crowd, for how happy they are that a humble, deserving man—a worker among workers—has finally been recognized for his quiet strength. Consistent with his modest nature, the man appears to be embarrassed by both *#dunamisto*'s kind words and the crowd's reaction and, with the relief of the drowned man saved by the toss of a ring buoy, he embraces a woman who appears to be his adoring wife. I again assess this more aesthetically pleasing and compassionate version of the sculpture and am further convinced that the worker has implanted a conscience, a soul, into the thing's electrical bowels.

I am poised to walk across the street and confront my poisoners when I feel a hand on my right elbow. I fear, of course, that I may be mugged. Ready to invoke the self-defense tactics taught to me without success by my father, I turn to see not a street thief, but *Polsky*. He stands, as always, in all of his effete and pompous glory—dressed today in a grey and white seersucker suit and a broad panama hat fit for the owner of a hacienda.

"Bobby," he says, "I *thought* that was you."

"Ivan," I reply coolly, with not even the faintest interest in civility.

"How are you feeling?" he asks, his hand placed with condescension on my shoulder. "I was sorry to see you looking so ill the other day. Running oddly, with your legs so close together. Was that a muscle cramp? And then bent over at the waist? I hope you're okay, now. *Sorry.*"

There he goes again with his *sorry*! I am now even more livid with the papaya and hot dog shop, for not only did they cause me the most severe gastrointestinal distress, but they have also exposed me to Polsky's insufferable ridicule. To make the clearest point, I do not respond to his insincere words. Rather, I make a remark about the beauty of the weather, for is there a more potent way to convey one's disinterest than discussing the weather? (It happens to be a lovely day—warm but not humid, with a high sun and a gentle breeze that flows off the river.) I believe that Polsky is aware of my clever ploy, for now *he* does not respond to *my* insincere words. We are not unlike two quarreling lovers who refuse to given even a fraction of an inch.

Polsky points over to the sculpture. "Amazing," he says. "Whether you like it or not—as art, I mean—you have to admire what it evokes in people. Look at this crowd."

I scan the plaza and observe the scores of people who examine the sculpture, photograph it, run their hands over its smooth metal skin, frown and laugh, nod and scratch their heads. These people are indeed engaged.

"Yes," I say, reluctant to validate Polsky's observation, "yes, it is amazing."

"Have you been in?" he asks.

I do not know what he means, and I maintain vigilance for fear that he may be guiding me into a repartee that will leave me embarrassed and fuming. "Been in?"

"Yes, inside the sculpture. Under it. Have you gotten a reading?"

I recall Helen Schweitzer, the waddling woman who was denounced for her diet of fatty foods and was revealed to have an unsatisfying sexual life. I wonder now if she was merely a talented actor—as I thought at the time—or if she was in actuality an earnest participant humiliated by the truth of #dunamisto's analysis. "I have not," I reply.

Polsky looks aghast, as if I had just admitted that I have never eaten an oyster. (I am ashamed to admit that I have never eaten an oyster, and the reason I have never done so is because they, at the moment of consumption, are not only raw but *alive!*)

"Well, you must," he says. "I did it the other day and the results were remarkable. How it gathers this information is astounding—the things it knows about a human being. It listed my many accolades, *the MacArthur*, my competitive spirit, my flair—and it even accused me of having a penchant for playing politics! That I don't agree with—the politics—but everything else was spot on." As he looks over to the sculpture and furrows his brow, I recall my father's outrage at Polsky's departmental treachery, how this snob undermined a talented rival's quest for tenure. He removes the panama hat and with a kerchief wipes his sweaty forehead. "An amazing thing, this sculpture. You should think about trying it yourself, Bobby."

I pull my cap—my father's cap—down low over my brow. "Robert," I mutter, infuriated as always by his use of the diminutive. "Robert."

He smiles wickedly and tightens his grip. "Come with me, *Robert*," he says and, with a bounce in his step, leads me by the elbow to the back of the line. "Give it a go, young man." And with that, he retreats back into the crowd. (The circumference of his panama hat is so great that the crowd parts to avoid its sharp edges.)

I stand in line and gaze up at the sculpture. The sunlight strikes the figure in such a way that a halo—a glowing, pollen-infused aureole that suggests some divine blessing—appears above its head. The once mutated face now appears peaceful, beatific, exuding a gravitational pull, as if I am being drawn into the safest, most welcoming maternal arms—into the arms of the Mother. As the line shortens, I step forward, moving closer to some communion with this work of art—and, possibly, with an existential question long unanswered.

One after the next, people step into *#dunamisto*'s void, await the flurry of digital fireworks, and then emerge to view the extent of this creation's insight; one after the next, these brave souls appear both shocked and pleased with the words displayed on the huge screen. I am profoundly moved when the young boy in front of me exits to see that *#dunamisto* has recognized in him a great but unrealized musical talent. "See!" the boy yells to his embarrassed mother, "I *told* you I could be good." I smile, for how encouraging, how nurturing this being has become— how, like its human equivalents, it has developed the capacity for change. (I think of Stavros and his newfound affection for homosexuals.)

My turn has arrived, and the uniformed guard directs me into *#dunamisto*'s cavity. I proceed with neither excitement nor dread, but rather with a sense of serenity. As I step into the triangular gap, I reach up and run my hands over the metal skin, which like the hood of an idling automobile is warm to the touch. I notice that there is a slight vibration in the metal surface, and I wonder if this tremor is the result of the subway trains below or the inner workings of *#dunamisto*. The guard nods to me, an indication that I should proceed with a short statement about myself.

It is this imminent disclosure that causes me to recall an upsetting story from my youth. I was no more than eight when my mother descended into one of her dark moods, and so despondent was she that, after psychiatrists failed to lift her spirits, she sought the counsel of a fortune-teller. This woman, a crafty Roma and con artist, was able to extract from my mother so much personal information—emotional, familial, financial, and otherwise—that she robbed my parents of a considerable fortune. How furious was my father—how exasperated by her mental condition and the havoc it wreaked upon us all. And how my mother slipped into an even deeper depression after the cost of her naïveté was calculated.

Thus, concerned about the risks of revealing too much information and also desiring to test the full capabilities of *#dunamisto*'s intuition, I provide only the most minimal disclosure.

"My name is Robert and I live in New York."

The crowd erupts in laughter, for I have offered such

scant data that the likelihood of an accurate analysis seems impossible. I, like the waddling Helen Schweitzer before me, smile coyly. I look up to the screen and see the explosions of red, white, and blue: the Roman candle, the falling leaf, the peony, the strobe. The pyrotechnics, which normally last no more than several seconds, continue to dazzle for ten, twenty, thirty seconds—a minute. I place my hand to the beast's metal skin and feel that both the heat and the vibration have intensified. Fearful that *#dunamisto* has reached its functional limits and may explode atop me, I step out into the light, my eyes still trained on the giant screen above. At last the screen goes dark, and the crowd and I share a gasp of anticipation. I watch as words begin to form on the screen, and with the realization of each word, I experience what feels like an arrhythmia of the heart, the skipping of a precious beat, as if the days of my life are reducing in number.

"Bobby Walser," *#dunamisto* declares, "the crux of your predicament is this: no matter how hard you try, you can never be your father—and you will always be your mother."

I stare in disbelief at the words before me, before the crowd of onlookers. As if punched in the solar plexus, I struggle to breathe. I rub my eyes and read again. The words now confirmed, I feel as if a heavy hand has gripped my throat. My eyes tear and my lips swell. A vein throbs on my forehead. But the most painful reaction to *#dunamisto*'s verdict is not physical: it is my spirit that is wounded, for I recognize in these words not just the possibility of truth, but the very *certainty* of truth.

I think about my father, Kingsley Walser—war hero, physicist, minor league baseball player, distinguished professor, and writer who was short-listed for several prestigious awards. I think about my own small life, comparing it unfavorably to the vastness of his. I recall not only his great love for me, but his nagging fear that I had inherited my mother's darkness and her pageantry, her inability to exist in the world such as it is. I again recall with a shiver the boxing lessons that he gave me after I was bullied in school, when he led me to the driveway and demonstrated to me the proper technique for defending oneself against physical violence (and imposing it upon others). There I was, my arms flailing in the most uncoordinated way, unable to make full contact with the hands that he held out as targets—and I recall with the most exquisite clarity the look of terror on my father's face, one that confirmed a father's most ghastly fear: that his son lacked the tools necessary to survive in this brutal world.

I look up at the sculpture, whose head has returned to its twisted and mutated form, blanketed again with a chilling mask of authority. I cannot bear to look at this metal beast and thus divert my attention to the crowd. In the front row, I see Polsky's panama hat—and below it Polsky himself. This man, who knew my father well, waves to me solemnly. "Sorry," he mouths. And I believe that he forms this word with sincerity, as though even he understands the gravity of what has just occurred. I nod in appreciation for his sympathy. "Goodbye," he says and disappears into the crowd.

Given what has just transpired, I abandon my plan to confront the hot dog poisoners and, my legs as heavy as wet rope, trudge instead toward the river, considering the words of *#dunamisto* as I go. I wonder if my whole life has been formed by my inability to be the man my father was, to achieve even a fraction of what he had achieved. And I wonder if this inability has led to an inescapable sense of inferiority, one that in turn caused me to mimic my mother, the parent whose personality came so naturally to me and whose modest accomplishments were within my limited grasp. Is it possible, I wonder, that the desire to equal or exceed a parent—*either* parent—is so strong that we will follow him or her to the grave without ever understanding the tragic path that we have chosen? Or is there no such impetus? Is one's outcome merely a matter of genetics? Of wiring? A makeup that has ignored the special heredity of one and instead reproduced the weakened genome of the other, one that for centuries has somehow escaped the filtering forces of natural selection?

I reach the southern tip of Riverside Park, a mere hundred feet from my building's entrance. Rather than return to my apartment and slide under the cool sheets of my bed, I decide to take a stroll in the lush park. It is now the middle of the afternoon and I am fatigued from the events of the day, saddened by the words of that despicable, repugnant thing, that cheapest imitation of art. I have not the desire to try to understand how that monster could say such a thing, whether its intuition was based on some horrifying algorithm or if the beast merely generated random statements that by chance happened to resonate with me. But then I recall that the metal demon uttered my surname, thus refuting the notion of some blind luck, and it is this realization that makes me long for a simpler time—for the Russia of Chekhov, perhaps.

I walk no more than ten blocks through the park and am stricken with a paralyzing fatigue. I sit on a bench and look out over the water, which appears even more grim than usual. Its color, once a cheerless grey, now resembles a channel of slick petroleum—black and viscous. The white caps, still reminiscent of the noxious reynard's scissor-sharp teeth, rise from the water's slithery surface and remain upright, stiff. At this moment, the river seems to me less a fluid in motion and more a painting, a snapshot, a still life, a bleak moment fixed in time.

As the sun threatens to plant the most delicate kiss on the Jersey skyline, my fatigue becomes so great that I have not the energy to keep my eyes open or to rise and return home. I look around the park and see only a young mother with her freckled child and, in the distance, two lovers welded in a passionate embrace. (Oh how I long to be like them, to embrace my steampunk goddess on the banks of the Schuylkill River.) My exhaustion is now so potent that I lie down on the bench. Giving little thought to my own safety, I pull my cap—my father's cap—over my face and close my eyes, drifting in an instant into a deep sleep.

When I awaken some time later, I am unsure of the passage of time, but what is clear to me is that night has fallen. The bleak river is no longer visible, although in the darkness I can still hear its muffled roar and inhale its brackish smell. I look around to see that I am alone in the park and that I am only partially illuminated by a nearby streetlamp, a flickering thing that emits a wan and diluted light. I reach for my vest, for the fob of my gold pocket watch—and am shocked to realize that my antique timepiece is missing! As if trying to prove that I am experiencing nothing more than a terrifying nightmare, I pick at the fabric of my vest, hoping that I am somehow mistaken. But the barren cloth does not lie, and I am sick, for this is the very watch that my father wore during my performance of *The Cherry Orchard*, the one he held when he fell dead into the center aisle—the same one that counted down his final minutes, his final *seconds*.

Panicked, I reach for my interior jacket pocket—and find that my wallet too is missing! And with it, the photograph of my dear Rose at the steampunk cotillion has also disappeared. I am consumed with self-loathing and the agony of losing a cherished item, for how could a man so blessed be so careless? How could the recipient of such largesse betray a divine woman through a lack of the most basic vigilance? (Alas, how unworthy I am of her love.)

I sit up on the bench and reach for my head, for my father's cap. My head is bare, uncovered, and my heart races with the recognition of yet another loss, but then I look to the ground and see the mud-scuffed cap below— and I experience a great exultation. With considerable care and appreciation, I lift the cap from the dirt. I brush it off and place it atop my head—a soothing connection to the great Kingsley Walser, the man whom I shall never be. I then look down and examine my state. Given the magnitude of what I have just lost, I am pleased to be wearing my shoes, my ostrich belt, my clothing—and I am relieved, of course, to have retained both of my kidneys. (Our mayor is so disinterested in fighting crime that a gang of Albanian organ harvesters is rumored to run rampant through our parks and alleyways, and I believe they stole a kidney from a napping poet in Prospect Park.)

I am poised to rise from the bench and trudge home when I see something in the distance, something unusual yet familiar in a marshy patch. Before me is a hazy light, undulating and vaporous, that emits a turquoise hue. The beat of my heart quickens, for I see before me something resembling the fool's fire, the *ignis fatuus*, the will-o'-the-wisp from so many years ago. I recall that evening, on the anniversary of my mother's birth, when my father and I sat on the back porch and gazed out to the thick swamp, transfixed by those inexplicable glowing lights. I recall my father's explanation of this phenomenon—that my dead mother was paying us a visit, reminding us of her great love. I think about the many years during which I would search for these same lights and my profound sadness when they did not take form.

I picture now the moment when I found my mother swaying from the bathroom ceiling, how I held her tight, how I screamed for my father—and how I was crushed under the weight of her dead body. My thoughts turn to a recollection of my mother's kindness. In particular, I again recall how she comforted me when I feared, even as a young boy, that a girl would never condescend to date me, that a woman would never marry me—that I would never be loved. "Robert," she said, "you *will* find someone … and if not, you'll always have me." A tear forms in my eye, for I must now admit that it was she—and not my father—whom I was meant to follow. I picture the words of #*dunamisto* on the screen, and I accept the devastating truth—that I have spent an entire lifetime chasing the wrong light.

I watch as the will-o'-the-wisp pulsates and glows in the darkness. The sinuous, ethereal light beckons me, seduces me, draws me into its phosphorescent power. I recall the folklore of these swamp lights, how they entice travelers with their siren's glow, then lure them to deaths most gruesome. But despite this frightening legend, I walk without fear toward the light—toward *my mother*. And with each step, I move closer to a most otherworldly reunion.

I am now no more than five feet from this radiant apparition, and just as I am about to step into its warm, placental glow there is a great burst of light and a heat so strong that I fear my skin has been burned—and then there is nothing. The light has been extinguished, and all that I see before me is the darkness and the oily river with its white-capped fangs. I wave my hand through the air, through the area where the light just glowed, but feel only the residual heat of some now extinguished soul.

I weep, for I have lost my mother—again.

I am broken, unfixable. I look around the empty park and notice the silhouette of a garbage can near the bench on which I earlier slept. I cross the grass and reach for the receptacle, which is filled with trash. I turn it on its side, emptying the garbage onto the ground. With considerable effort, I then drag the waste bin across the grass and, when I have reached a point just below a maple's wiry branch, I turn the bin upside down so that its solid base faces the sky. I again look around the park. A shadowy figure darts through the brush—a dog, perhaps? Or Polsky? The rays of a half moon peek through the maple's leaves. A moaning sound, a plaintive howl, echoes off the water. (Is that Luna's mournful hamster howl?) I climb atop the trashcan and reach up to the branch. I pull down on it to test its strength. Satisfied, I unbuckle my ostrich belt and withdraw it from the loops around my waist. I then wrap the open belt around my neck and run its tip back through the buckle, creating a noose-like loop. My penultimate act of engineering is to tie the belt's remaining length around the supporting branch.

I stare out to the inert river. My thoughts turn to my beloved Rose, and another sad reality occurs to me. I concede that I shall never see her, that there will be no trip to Philadelphia, no walks along the river, no tender embrace—no snapped garter belt and no Buck Rogers laser gun. I concede that my love for Rose is just another of my follies, another in a long history of delusions great and small: in this case, the insane delusion that I could both love *and* be loved. I picture my sweet dove, how she suffers the most debasing adversity with the grace of an angel, how she refuses to let the pains of this hard life cripple her. And despite my great love for her, I take some comfort in the prospect that her life will be better without me—for this steampunk girl is the past *and* the future, while I am merely the past. I shuffle my feet on the metal grate of the garbage can. *I love you, Rose.*

With my right hand, I tighten the belt around my neck. My thoughts turn to the moment my great father died. I picture myself on stage in the role of Boris Borisovich Simeonov-Pishchik, the fading aristocrat who is supremely confident that some great fortune will come his way. I recall a scene near the end of the fourth and final act, a point in the play that we did not reach because of my father's tragic and untimely death. Pishchik, against the greatest of odds, has indeed come into a small fortune. (An Englishman, of course, has discovered on the aristocrat's property a vein of valuable minerals.) After revealing his good luck to his stunned comrades, this character relates an odd story that has intrigued me, haunted me, from my very first reading. "A young man," says Pishchik, "just described how some brilliant philosopher encourages everyone to jump from a roof. 'Go and jump,' he tells them, 'and your problems will be solved.'"

I look down at the ground below me, which is no more than four feet away. I wonder if this act will cure me, if it will solve my problem. I think about my particular problem: the past. I recall the look of unspeakable terror on my father's face when he realized that I, his young son, failed to possess the most basic tools necessary to survive in this modern world—and I weep for every ineffectual child who has witnessed in a parent this look of unspeakable terror.

An anger now rises within me, for I wonder if it is not the sad events of my childhood that have destroyed me, but instead modernity itself that has taken a deadly toll. For what I now see is a modernity that has refused to tolerate my temporal dislocation, whatever its cause— and a modernity that, too, has refused to tolerate even the most minor eccentricities in my fellow man. And as I consider the tyranny of this intolerance, I wonder, is it not the present—and the future, too—that has driven me to this tragic point? (Or is it I alone who is responsible?)

These thoughts of present and future again lead me to consider the diabolical sculpture. I think about the thing's mutated head and its soulless mass, its ability to transmogrify from malignant to benign and back again, and to know things that should not be known. Other than inflicting the deepest psychic pain on its admirers (poor Helen Schweitzer and her fictitious hypothyroidism), I wonder what this thing does with the information it gathers—what the trio of unlikely patrons does with the conclusions drawn by its creation. Perhaps its very goal is to inflict this psychic pain (*you can never be your father—and you will always be your mother*) and then sell to us a spurious balm to heal our wounds. Or perhaps its goal is to destroy us. Or both.

I experience an ache in my chest. *Go and jump*, I think, *and your problems will be solved*. And as I feel the pinch of the belt against my neck, I wonder what has become of me—of *us*. I face southeast, in the general direction of *#dunamisto*. I wave goodbye to *#dunamisto*. I extend my middle finger to this deranged monstrosity. "Fuck you!" I yell. "*Fuck. You.*" (Oh how I adored the spirited girl on the courthouse steps.)

And then, with the belt tight around my neck, I raise my right foot and prepare to step off the side of the trash can. I prepare for the belt's grip against my skin. I prepare for my final breath. But before I do so, before my final voluntary act, I notice a movement on the ground below. Not far from me, a small rodent rummages through a mound of refuse. The creature pauses amidst the trash as if a great idea has formed in its tiny brain. And with the glassiest eyes, this kind thing looks up and offers me its twitching nose. I recall the moment when those hooligans, those heartless private schoolers, stole Luna's ashes, and my heart pounds with rage. As if we have once met, as if we are the oldest of friends, this gentle being raises a pink paw and blinks. Luna? I ask. And my question is answered, for this angelic creature nods with an affirmation, with an immortal spirit that suggests to me the possibility of reincarnation—and then it scampers away.

Unaware now of the passage of time, I look around the park. I believe that hours have passed and that morning nears, for the sky to the east has turned a lavender blue with streaks of the most ethereal white. I imagine *#dunamisto* to the east—its malignant head, its twisted vortex of a mouth sucking from the sky, from the world, all that is beautiful. With great resolve, I again lift my foot and prepare to step into the void. The belt tightens around my neck. I gasp for air. And as I am about to leave this tortured earth, I recall another Jewish prayer—one that I first heard in the saddest film, one that took place during the closing days of the Second World War. *Sh'ma Yisrael, Adonai Eloheinu, Adonai Echad.*

"Goodbye," I say. And as I lower my right leg over the side, as I prepare to join my dear mother and father in an eternity that must surely transcend this world in which I live, something catches my attention in the distance, not far from the water's edge. I again see the fool's fire, *ignis fatuus*, will-o'-the-wisp—but this time the glowing lights are not my mother. What I see instead is my steampunk goddess in an illuminated form! My dear Rose—celestial, gossamer, vaporous—a pulsating beacon that beckons me, calls out to me, pleads with me not to take that lethal step. I place my foot back down on the garbage can, and as I do so, the will-o'-the-wisp explodes in a supernova of such radiant brilliance that I must cover my eyes.

From the water's edge, emanating from within this explosion of light, I hear a voice—the angelic voice of my beloved Rose. "Today," she sings, as if calling out to every suffering creature. *"Today."* I recall her generous invitation, her plea that I visit her in Philadelphia, the indignities my poor angel must endure. So uplifted am I by this image before me and by her spoken word, so inspired by her love, that a transformation occurs within me—the deepest and most profound shift. And it is this tectonic shift that causes me to raise my hand and loosen the belt. As if guided by some kind and compassionate creator, I withdraw my head from the loop and, with the grace and agility of the lithest ballerino, leap from the garbage can.

My feet now on terra firma, I maneuver through the park and, possessed by the speed of some wild beast, sprint south. And with each fluid stride my heart beats—and it does so with the hope of the living, with the hope of the good man pardoned by Mercy, with the thunderous hope of a young nation.

"Rose," I howl to the brightening sky. "Here I come. *Today!*"

Eleven

With nervous anticipation, I peer out the window and watch as the train car sluices through the pungent, gurgling swamps of northern New Jersey. I wonder what glides below the surface of the smooth brown water; what hides beneath the dense, primordial muck; what gems and horrors, what creatures great and small slither through the silt while the frantic world whirls above. I recall the last time I visited the great city of Philadelphia—a wintry day when I was a child, when my father delivered a lecture at the University of Pennsylvania, when I sat in the rear of the classroom and reveled in the brilliance of Dr. Kingsley Walser. I recall the young graduate student who approached him after the lecture, how she blushed and curtseyed in a manner that made my father smile.

A great weariness now consumes me, a fatigue so deep and heavy that I have no choice but to surrender to its power. I think of Rose, how she will greet me at 30th Street Station—an august terminal worthy of its stately role in the City of Brotherly Love. I glance out the window and notice a heron sailing mere feet above the slick, brown water, the tips of its white wings tickling the swampy liquid. Lovestruck, I close my eyes—and awake two hours later as the train enters the station, my heart pattering, my circuitry run amok.

From my bag I remove a lint brush and roll it over my velvet lapels, lifting from the fabric a few wayward hairs and some irksome fuzz. Satisfied, I rise to exit the train car, my spirits exalted by the imminence of this union with Rose. A gaggle of fellow passengers has amassed in front of the sliding doors, and I curse the delay that this throng will cause me, for each second that now prolongs my separation from Rose is a second of the greatest distress. I fear that any delay, any suggestion to her that I have not accepted her gracious offer of a visit, will trigger flight in her skittish soul. But like the pent-up waters rushing through a ruptured dam, the crowd disperses in an unexpected flash, and I am granted passage. Delighted, I skip out of the car and gallop down the platform.

When I emerge seconds later in the station's grand chamber, I look around for Rose, for my beautiful steampunk goddess. Before me stand several women, all dressed in the conventional feminine garb of our times: smart dresses, professional suits, and muted tones. Amused by their slavish adherence to modern convention, I search the crowd. My search, though, is soon interrupted by the sight of a glorious bronze sculpture: a thirty-foot-high work of art, one that depicts Michael the Archangel, the angel of resurrection, lifting a heroic soldier from the dead. And as I marvel at the sculpture's majesty, I consider the cold brutalism of *#dunamisto*. I think about the past of this angel and then the future of *#dunamisto*—the present of it, really—and my distaste for anything but golden yore is further reinforced.

I again scan the grand hall in search of Rose. I see no one dressed in the alluring steampunk attire—no corsets or prairie skirts, no brass monocles or laser guns. My shoulders slouch in familiar rejection, and as I look around this terminal I find that its great architectural attributes too slouch in a manner that suggests defeat, an understanding that its proportions, columns, light, and flow all pale in comparison to the great edifices of Europe. The majestic pillars buckle under the weight of the leaden roof; the mullioned windows repel the sun's light; the marble beneath my feet sheds its glimmer and turns into a dull slurry.

"Fool," I mutter, audible only to me. "*Fool*," I bark loudly, audible to a vigilant mother and her alarmed young daughter. I recall the mother and child from the shop that sells hot dogs and papaya juice, how they suspected me of sinister intentions. I shudder, and I do so at my propensity to alarm even the most innocent and accepting of creatures, those delightful little cherubs who blush in my presence and clutch their mother's skirts in fear of I know not what.

I look up to a large sign, one that announces both comings and goings. I note that in ten minutes a train will depart this foul station for an even fouler terminal in New York. Awash in humiliation, I reach for the return ticket in my trouser pocket. I am at last forced to concede that I am a man who has not only clung to the most foolish delusion, but who has encouraged it, nurtured it, given life to the illusory. I have created the fantasy of a union where even the densest, most quixotic man would see rejection. As I trudge back to the gate, toward yet another lonely voyage, I pause and turn to admire for the last time the *Angel of the Resurrection.*

Before I reach the gate, though, I gasp—for beneath the glorious metal sculpture now stands another angel of the most transcendent form. There, illuminated by a column of milky light, is a woman in a ruby-colored Victorian dress with an exposed silk corset. She wears lace gloves and sports a monocle over her right eye. An oversized pocket watch dangles from her hip. As if drawn by some irresistible force, I glide toward this woman. I examine her face, which bears some resemblance to the photograph of Rose. My heart beats again with the thunderous hope of a young nation. I raise my hand—a wave, a prayer, part honorific, part hopeful—to this woman.

The woman takes a tentative step toward me. She too raises her hand—and she appears to catch a throbbing beam of sunlight, which settles like a fireball in her tiny palm. I gasp. Pleased, she smiles like the adroit magician who has just dazzled a baffled crowd.

"Robert?" she says and takes yet another step in my direction. She closes her fist, extinguishing the fireball in her palm. "Robert? Is it really ...?"

I thank the gods for their great kindness, for their compassion. "Yes, yes," I say, "It is I."

Rose smiles and darts toward me. She throws her slender arms around me. She whinnies like a nervous foal and presses her lovely face into the crook of my neck. "I'm sorry," she whispers, "so sorry for what I did to ya ... never showin' up. Thanks for comin'. Thanks so much."

She speaks in a manner—colloquial and ironic—that

causes me to giggle. I laugh at what must be an indication of her humor, a purposeful contortion of the English language, a tip of the hat to the value I have long placed on eloquence and proper diction. She squeezes my hand, and I think about the many times I trekked on foot to the Port Authority, the sadness I would feel each time Rose failed to step from the bus; I recall those moments when I questioned my sanity, wondering if I were suffering from some traumatic brain injury, some creeping dementia, a psychopathology manifesting in the most insane delusions; and I recall the lonely carriage ride home, with the mutton-chopped driver, his black top hat and his temporal dislocation.

"There is no need to apologize, Rose, for you have endured so much."

"Oh, Robert, I been waitin' so long for today." She turns and points to the southern end of the grand terminal. "Come with me! This way. My car's 'round the corner. Right over there."

We skip across the glossy marble floor, synchronized as if we have enacted this same cinematic spectacle for decades—two people, united, co-joined in the most perfect cadence. We emerge from the station, this cathedral to our miraculous love, and Rose guides me to her automobile. Given her steampunk aesthetic, I am expecting some creative combination of past and future—perhaps a 1935 Chrysler Airstream with whitewall tires and, on the roof, brass lightning bolts and a series of high-tech centrifuges.

"Over here," she says. She points to an automobile, one that surprises me with its modesty, with its origins not in the past or the future, but in some not too distant present. She has paused before a small, yellow vehi-cle—Japanese or Korean, I believe—with a dent on the passenger's door. I manage to hide my surprise, then dart around to the driver's side and, in my chivalrous way, open the door for her. "Thanks," she says.

"You are most welcome," I reply. Once she is settled in her seat, I close the door with great care and proceed to walk around the front of the car. Waving to her as I pass, I situate myself in the passenger's seat and run my hand across the dusty dashboard. I look down to the polished leather of my loafers and see on the floor below several discarded wrappers from a fast food chain; I notice a bent French fry near the tip of my right shoe.

"Whatcha wanna do?" she asks. "Indepen'ence Hall? Rit'house Square? A Philly chee'steak?" I wonder how long my love shall commit to her diction, how long she shall engage—with tongue firmly implanted in cheek—in this breezy vernacular. She reaches over, lambently taps my left hand, then withdraws and grips the steering wheel—and this brief contact, this fleeting tactility, acts as an opiate that flushes through my starving veins.

"I would most enjoy a stroll … on the campus of the University of Pennsylvania, perhaps," I say, recalling my father's lecture there on the subject of our nation's insid-ious de facto aristocracy and the importance of upward mobility among all classes.

"Never been there, but let's go," Rose replies. "'S up on Walnut, right?"

"Yes, yes my love," I say, "It is up on Walnut. Walnut Street."

Rose lifts her leather boot from the brake and accel-erates west toward the campus. We drive in silence for several blocks, and I find that I am experiencing a heightened level of anxiety. When I glance to my left and observe Rose's alabaster skin peering out from her bodice, I recall the time when I closed my eyes in bed and imagined her in my passionate embrace, when a tumescence arose and transported me to some distant utopia. I enjoy these sensual thoughts for a few moments and then, sickened by my prurience, by my base urges, grip the handle of the passenger door and gaze out at the passing buildings.

"Wooter?" she asks.

"Excuse me?" I reply.

She points to a bottle of water in the automobile's center console. "Wooter, silly."

I laugh loudly and slap my right thigh in appreciation of her cleverness. "So kind of you," I say and take the bottle in my hand.

Within minutes, Rose has parked the car deftly within feet of the university, and we walk arm in arm toward the campus. As we cross Walnut Street and enter this urban oasis, not far from the university's library, I notice something about Rose that surprises me and that has the effect of further enhancing my adoration for her: my angel, I have just realized, walks with a limp. I look down to the ground and observe her awkward gait, the peculiar inward curve of her right foot, the thickness of her sole, the choppiness of her step.

Consumed with the most tender feelings for her and for the hardships she must endure, I grip her arm tightly and guide her into the heart of the campus. There, on the very lawn where the great Benjamin Franklin strolled and pondered the mysteries of life, Rose and I sit in something approximating quiet contemplation. I watch as the students dart about on the cobbled paths, their soft faces painted with nervous ambition.

"Nice to just look 'round at all the pretty buildin's," she says.

My heart races, not from some divinely inspired joy, but from a burgeoning anxiety—from the fear that Rose is not, in fact, affecting a casual vernacular for my amusement; I fear that this is how she really speaks.

"Rose," I say in my most courteous and respectful manner, "this way that you speak. Is … is it …?"

Rose winces, and I sense in her a painful shift. She reaches for my hand and slowly lowers herself down to the grass, bringing me with her. Here we lie, our shoulders touching, our fingers now intertwined, gazing up to the miraculous sky: a crisp blue, a blob of sun, with one proud cloud shaped like a lamb or a tractor or a cup of tea. I grip Rose's hand as if I am trying to prevent her from slipping into some dark and voluminous void. I look down to my feet, to her feet, and observe the curvature of her right foot, the thick rubber sole. I release my grip and stroke her arm, and I do so with such tenderness that I ache.

Rose wriggles closer to me and rests the back of her head on my shoulder. She looks upward and points to the sky, to the cloud shaped like a lamb or a tractor or a cup of tea.

"Look at that cloud," she says with the glee of a child. "So beeyoodiful!"

The sun infuses me with its warmth and with feelings of the greatest contentment. I smile—and I do so with the freedom, with the liberty, with the unconsciousness that is birthed by the complete, unqualified acceptance of another human being.

"It is," I reply, cursing myself for my pretentious judgment of her colloquialisms. I think about my father and his love for our nation's many regional dialects—each one the idiosyncratic result of generations of socio-economic and linguistic influences. I rage against my arrogance and, as Rose grasps my hand, I find myself at peace with every aspect of this woman, with every difference between us. "It's *beeyoodiful*," I say.

Rose lifts her head from my shoulder and looks at me. She strokes my cheek and smiles in a way that conveys the very depths of her miraculous character. Her eyes are moist.

"Thanks," she says. "Thanks for that. For talkin' like me." She places her head, the side of her face, on my chest. She rests her crooked right foot on my leg. And I thank the gods.

Twelve

My mood on the train ride back to New York later this day is so exalted that I feel as though I am in communion with every living thing, both fauna and flora. In fact, so great is my affection for the passengers, those peculiar types who would normally irk me, that they now delight me with their eccentricities and foibles. As I look out the window and gaze at the shimmering water in the distance, I recall the magical day with my beloved. There was that beautiful moment on the university lawn, followed by cheesesteaks on South Street. (How those greasy meat sandwiches rival in popularity the delicacies of the hot dog and papaya stand!) Rose and I then walked together, arm in arm, to Independence Hall, where I found myself so moved by the sacrifices of our founding fathers that I nearly wept with gratitude—the type reserved for the man who is the most undeserved beneficiary of another human's genius.

I recall now the moment when Rose and I bid adieu, when we stood under the *Angel of the Resurrection* and hugged with desperation.

"Thanks for a glorious day," she said. "Simpahlee glorious. And next time I'm comin' to New York. Never been there, ya know. Never."

"Thank *you*," I replied. "It has been the highest honor for me to pass an afternoon with you, Rose. And I do hope that we shall see each other posthaste, either here or in New York."

As the train takes a bend north and proceeds along the New Jersey coast, I close my eyes. I revel in the warmth of my love, and I consider what I shall do upon my return to the city that both delights and confounds me. I think of Rose, of course, and how she represents all that is good in this world: kindness, humility, loyalty, perseverance, and the work ethic of a yak. In the distance, beside a cargo ship, there stands a row of colossal port cranes—giant metal monsters that in their menacing, inanimate power remind me of *#dunamisto*. I shiver at the thought of the sculpture, of its trenchant insight, its cruelty.

The train soon deposits me into that brutal subterranean sarcophagus known as Penn Station. As I traverse the enclosed vault in search of an exit, I notice a one-legged pigeon hopping about as if on hot coals. I look around the windowless cavern and wonder how it is possible that this bird has made its way so deep into the earth—and how it might ever be emancipated, how it might ever again take flight. I wonder if the pigeon might prefer to hobble about this terminal, rather than fly from ledge to ledge in the city above. My heart beating for the tragedy of this poor creature, I make my way up a set of stairs that leads toward the exit.

When I emerge from the terminal, I notice that

dozens of people wait in line for a taxi, and my thoughts thus turn to the possibility that I must endure yet another subway ride—and the further possibility that I may have to dislodge an able-bodied man so that a pregnant woman may sit. I decide instead to walk the two or so miles to my home, up Eighth Avenue, past the horrid Port Authority, and along the western edge of Times Square. So giddy am I with thoughts of my visit with Rose that I notice little of my surroundings and soon find myself at the intersection of 72nd and Broadway.

There, the metal beast looks down at the masses with its mechanized derision. I stare into the absent eyes of *#dunamisto* and recall the words uttered by its tortured, torturing algorithm, how it demeans the decent under the guise of brilliance, of advancement. I squint at the sculpture in a manner not unlike a dueling sheriff poised to draw his six-shooter. "We shall meet again," I declare to this sickening mass and tip my cap in sarcastic deference. "We shall meet again."

We pass the restaurant owned by Stavros. (It is closed, of course. In the heart of dinnertime, no less.) I eye a delicious bear claw in the window. Is that Stavros I see in the shadows? Lurking behind the counter? Doing god knows what in the dark and empty dining room? Perhaps.

When I arrive at my flat moments later, I see that the light on my answering machine blinks and my heart thus races with excitement. I tap the button, awaiting the voice and the message it carries.

"Robert, it's Belinda." My literary agent, the esteemed Belinda St. Clair, has resurfaced! She has to my great surprise not abandoned me, as I feared she would after my conflict with her nephew and after the journal in Medicine

Hat, Alberta declared bankruptcy and refused to publish my short story.

"I've got good news," she says in an unusually chirpy voice. "Great, in fact." I can hear her take a luxurious drag from a Winston Super Slim, her cigarette of choice. "That Canadian journal? Saskatchewan? Alberta? Fuck if I can remember what it's called. Journal of... journal of something. Short fiction? Fictive shorts? They all sound the same. Anyway, it's not broke anymore. Turns out some writer—Brooklyn, of course—a pompous ass who had a huge hit—unwarranted, I thought it was rubbish—but anyway, he hit it big and wants some credibility, I guess. Literary status, blah, blah, blah. Nothing worse than a rich, insecure writer. So he put up a pile of money and saved the journal, which means your story's back on. It's going to run soon. Fall, winter, spring, maybe summer, next fall... We'll see. But your check's in the mail, as they say. Three hundred dollars—before my cut, of course." Belinda St. Clair takes another drag of her Winston Super Slim and then hangs up the phone.

I think about my characters—Lars and Lieke—and my heart leaps with emotion for the brilliant Dutch counterfeiter who adores his troubled sister. I raise my fists to the heavens, for at last my talent been understood, appreciated, *validated*. A feeling of the greatest pride overcomes me, as I have at last been seen. I exist! And as I stand in my salon and look around at the mementos of a life long gone—my father's diary, his ebony walking stick, my mother's cherished first editions (how she loved Walker Percy)—I wonder what remarkable things I might have achieved were it not for my losses. I wonder about the impact of an irreparable rupture, an early break that occurs before one is prepared for it, and the consequences that result. I wonder about the resilience of man, our ability, our drive to continue onward despite the tragedies we shall inevitably suffer. I wonder about my father and my mother. I consider their suffering. I *feel* their suffering. I eye the answering machine. And I whisper, "Can you see me now? Mom, Dad, can you see me now?"

Thirteen

A week has passed since my trip to Philadelphia, since that glorious day spent with my dear Rose. Invigorated by all that is good in the world, I open the front door of my flat and look down to the mat below. There, I see a multitude of invoices—many overdue—which causes in me a sense of dread and hopelessness. From beneath the pile of bills, though, I notice the crinkled corner of an envelope made from the finest parchment. I bend down and, as if the envelope were a plump, dewy flower, snatch it. I read the return address and see that—yes!—I have received a letter from Rose. I press the envelope to my lips, to the tip of my nose—and there it is. *Patchouli!*

Rather than tear open the envelope (as is my eager instinct), I instead repair to my study and lift from the desk the sterling letter opener given to me by my father. As I slip the sharp tip under the folded edge, I recall his words when I first clutched the knife: "The most civilized way to open an envelope—and with the added benefit of a soothing *swoosh* sound." I slice through the parchment, releasing a few fine fibers that drift upward through a shaft of amber light, hover for a moment in mid-air, then dart away as if chased by the wind. I remove the folded parchment and flatten it out on the surface of my desk, then adjust my lapels in deference to my delightful letter writer.

> Dearest Robert, Not for a moment since your departure have I failed to appreciate the kindness and generosity that you brought to me. I recall with true warmth those hours we strolled along the boulevards of Philadelphia and how we ate tasty cheesesteaks, one of the many brilliant delicacies my city has to offer. At the train station, I revealed to you with shame that I had never visited your great city, and you were sensitive enough not to belittle me for my provincial ways. So it is with great pride that I write you with wonderful news, my dear. I am coming to New York to visit you, Robert! On our walk you confided in me your love of Russian writers, so I took the liberty of purchasing two orchestra tickets for *The Cherry Orchard*. You shall be my date for the matinee on Sunday. I shall see you then, my love, in front of the theater. With greatest affection, Rose

My hands atwitch, I think not of the imminent and joyful reunion with my love, but of the play that I have avoided assiduously since my father's death. I curse my misfortune—the most remote chance that Rose would have unwittingly chosen the one play that troubles me so. My forehead dampens, and I experience a constriction in the throat that can only indicate influenza or anaphylaxis—or perhaps anxiety. I consider dialing the Doctor Kilkenny, but recall the quackery with which he distinguished himself when I was in the throes of some rare ailment. Instead I decide to walk to the barbershop and have a shave in anticipation of Rose's arrival.

The shop is empty except for the Cypriot Turk who reads the newspaper in a long white smock. Resembling a butcher or a surgeon or a high priest, the Turk points to an empty chair and tosses the paper into a sink. I watch as the water from the sink absorbs the paper, darkens it, and devours the words and photographs.

"Fucking Mets," the Cypriot says. "Fucking Mets. They're killing me. Can't pitch. Can't hit. Can't do anything. Same as always."

I recall my most recent foray into this very shop, when the barber and Stavros rued the performance of a baseball team to which they observed a strange and pitiful fealty.

"Fucking Mets," I say with a hint of shared grief, an attempt to gain the trust of this man before he presses a straight razor to my throat.

I settle into the seat, close my eyes, and soon feel the hot weight of a wet towel over my face.

"I guess it's a metaphor, right?" he says. "We care about some fucked up thing. Always think it's gonna get better, even though everyone's telling us it's time to move on." He massages my face through the towel. "Just one more, we say. One more month, one more season, one more crappy trip to the Rockaways, one more birthday, one more, one more, one more. And then you wake up a lifetime later—boy, it went fast. Your baseball team still sucks, your country's cut in half—goddamn Greeks—and me still giving a shave." He removes the hot towel from my face and looks down at me. "What's your thing?" he asks.

"My thing?"

In deep circular motions, he rubs shaving cream into my face. "The thing you won't let go of."

I look down to the tips of my polished shoes, to the cuffs on my shirt, the sterling links. I think about my father, the great Kingsley Walser. I recall my mother, how she dangled from the bathroom ceiling. I think about my refusal to let go of the past, my dogged insistence to live in the past. I look up to the Cypriot, who now holds a blade in his steady hand.

"I am attached to nothing," I pronounce, a lie that neither he nor I believes.

The next afternoon, I stand in front of the Lunt-Fontanne Theatre on West 46th Street and await the arrival of my gorgeous sparrow. I look up to the sign on the building's façade and read its ominous scarlet words: *The Cherry Orchard* by Anton Chekhov. I tremble in dread, in anticipation of what lies ahead; I tremble in delight, at the imminence of my reunion with Rose. I feel a tap on my shoulder and turn around—and there before me she stands.

"Robert!" she shrieks and throws her arms around me.

I clasp her tightly and, after a few exhilarating seconds, release and withdraw. Rose sports an ankle-length prairie skirt, a Buck Rogers–like gizmo on her right wrist, and a Victorian cameo pendant that dangles between her breasts.

"Rose, I'm so happy to see you. You look beautiful." I clear my throat. "Beeyoodiful!" I say.

She smiles, takes my hand and guides me into the theater. Inside, I catch a glimpse of a man who bears a resemblance to none other than the imperious Doctor Kilkenny, and I wonder again about the man's diagnostic acumen. This Kilkenny doppelganger looks at me, and I sigh in relief for it is not he (this man has a straighter nose and trustworthy eyes). Rose and I turn down the center aisle toward our seats, and I now notice another familiar theatergoer! This one looks not unlike Stavros. *Impossible*, I think—for a man of his questionable judgment and character could not possibly enjoy the finest theater. I wonder, though, if his recent appreciation for the rights of the gay and lesbian community has somehow enhanced his appreciation for Broadway shows. This man turns his full face to me, and I am surprised to see that it is not Stavros after all—but rather a man who shares only the Greek's bushy moustache. My heart races, and I wonder why I am so anxious, why I think I see men who have confounded me, these minor characters in my own life, who, I am ashamed to admit, bring out my most unattractive traits.

Rose examines the tickets and points to our seats. I count the aisles from the front of the theater and, to my horror, realize that we are sitting in the precise position where my father died: ninth row, center-right aisle. A film of sweat forms on my clammy forehead; my fingers twitch; a deep melancholy consumes me.

"Ya take the aisle," my cherub offers, as she sits down in the second seat.

Like the Cypriot barber who stared at me from above,

blade in hand, I look down to the seat below. *What's my thing?* I wonder, lowering myself to the cushion. *The thing I won't let go of.*

"So excitin'," Rose coos.

"Very," I reply, somewhat insincerely, and reach for her hand.

The housemaster extinguishes the lights, and, after a dramatic pause, the curtain rises. On the stage soon stand Madame Ranevskaya, Lopakhin, Pishchik, Firs, and others. The Madame, returned to Russia five years after the drowning death of her son, is in a precarious mental state, having just recently attempted suicide. I close my eyes and recall my own childhood participation in this drama, when my heart ached with possibility and beat with the love of my father. I hear now the voice of Boris Borisovich Simeonov-Pishchik, and I open my eyes to see the actor, the character, before me—center stage. This Pishchik wears a crimson velvet overcoat with an ermine collar, an embroidered silk waistcoat, and high, polished boots. He appears just as I did in my youth—and the passage of time, a thick mass of nostalgia and regret, fills my lungs. As Madame Ranevskaya speaks, I gasp, for I know what comes next—the lines immediately preceding my father's death.

Pishchik stands center stage. "Never surrender. How many times I've fretted, 'I'm finished. I cannot survive.' And then, out of nowhere, someone runs a railroad across my property and they pay me a fortune."

When the actor finishes his lines, I experience the most exquisite pain in my chest, and I wonder if I am suffering the same myocardial infarction that felled my father at this very moment. With little in the way of balance, I rise to my feet. I feel dear Rose reach for my hand as I turn toward the exit, away from Pishchik in his livery, and I dash out of the theater. Free from Rose's grasp, I burst through the rear curtains and sprint across the carpeted lobby to the doors that release out into the street. With the force of a firefighter, I lower my right shoulder into the door, causing it to blast open, and I fall into the street, enveloped in the air, the noise, the humanity. I kneel on the pavement; my heart races; I weep.

"Daddy!" I cry. "Daddy!" I am so bereft, so ashamed, that I cannot at this moment see the point in living. I wonder how I might take my own life, and I recall that moment in Riverside Park when I stood atop a garbage can, a belt around my neck, and contemplated my suicide, the release from suffering.

As I cry, my chest heaving, I feel upon my shoulder Rose's delicate hand. My shame is so great that I cannot look her in the eye. I am convinced that I do not deserve the affection of this great woman, and I fear that I shall bring her nothing but misery.

"Baby," she says, stroking my face. "What's wrong?"

I look up at the street before me. I consider running from her, running to the merciless river and diving into its fierce, inert waters.

"It's ... It's my father," I gasp. "*The Cherry Orchard* ... It's where he died ... in the middle of the play. Just then. Pishchik." I pause to gather myself. "When I was a child."

Rose envelops me. She whispers into my ear.

"I'm sorry, baby. So sorry. I had no idea. If I knew, I woulda taken ya to see a musical. Somethin' happy, with dancin' and songs." I look into her eyes. A tear glistens like a pearl beneath the glass of her bifocals. "You're my number one, Robert. *Number one.*"

I hear the sound of a horse's hooves on the pavement. To my great surprise, I look up to see the very same carriage, the very same driver, who first transported me home from the Port Authority. He wears the same black top hat, and his face is adorned with the same bushy muttonchops. He remains a man who has been transported from a distant era.

"Driver," I call out. "It is I, the man who gave you the bouquet of tulips just weeks ago." Rose looks at me in confusion. "Outside the Port Authority?" The man stares at me without even a glimmer of recognition. *Am I that unremarkable?* I wonder.

"Ride?" he says, pulling on the reins.

"A ride, yes," I reply through my tears. I lift Rose up onto the side step, and she slides across the leather bench. I soon join her, and we find ourselves shoulder to shoulder in something resembling an embrace.

"Seventy-second and West End," I say to the driver. "*Godspeed.*"

As we make our way up Eighth Avenue, Rose and I hold hands—and I find that her presence, her warmth, has the most therapeutic effect on me. I feel better in her arms, more hopeful, less rooted in the past. We say very little on our journey home, instead listening to the sounds of the horse, the driver, the carriage. We soon approach the dreadful intersection of 72nd and Broadway, and I experience a sense of foreboding unfamiliar to me since the moments before my mother's suicide. I wonder what could be the cause of this sensation, this intuition that something monumental, something catastrophic is imminent. Rose holds my hand as if she is afraid that I might take flight, and she does so with a protective determination that reminds me of my mother—and my father, too. To our left, just a hundred feet away, I see the hot dog and papaya shop, with its customary line of pleasure-seekers awaiting their fare. To the right stands the menacing sculpture.

"What's that?" Rose asks, pointing in the direction of *#dunamisto*.

I am fiercely protective of my love.

"That," I say, "is a monster. Art, science … a weapon of war. One or all of the above. Who knows? But I can say with assurance that it is a monster." I look at the base of the sculpture, at its spread legs, and I am relieved to see that no one stands beneath its vulgar groin. At this moment, no man has volunteered to be diagnosed by this thing, humiliated by it.

"It's not very pretty, is it?" my innocent creature asks. "Not pretty at all."

"No, it is not."

We come to a red light mere feet from the wicked sculpture, and I find that my instinct is to protect Rose from its wrath, to shield her from this monster. I turn my back to *#dunamisto* and wrap my arms around her, swaddling her in my love. With the scent of her perfume dancing through my nostrils, I experience such love for her that I feel as if I have never suffered loss, that my life has been a series of great gifts. Rose rests her chin on my shoulder, and I can sense her looking in the sculpture's direction, drawn in by its magnetic pull.

On the exterior wall of the subway station before me, I now see a parade of lights, intense reflections from a source that I fear is #*dunamisto*. I turn to see that yes, indeed, the monster's screen is flickering, its light-emitting diodes conjuring up some depraved attack on an innocent person. I am confused, though, for there is no one beneath its groin, no man, no woman naïvely volunteering to be eviscerated. Is it possible, I wonder, that #*dunamisto* has other victims in mind? Rose squeezes my hand.

"Go, driver, go," I yell. The light before us is red, and a taxi has pulled directly in front of our carriage, blocking our passage as it discharges passengers. "Dammit," I mutter. Concerned, I look over to the screen and see it twitching, bursting with pyrotechnics, *forming words*. As if Rose is a thoroughbred horse, I hold my hand up to her eyes, creating blinders to protect her from #*dunamisto*.

A mechanized voice claps across the plaza: "Rosemary Caputo," the creature bellows. I turn back to the sculpture, amazed that it now possesses a voice.

Rose pushes my hand away and stares in awe at #*dunamisto*. "How's it know my name?"

"Driver," I scream.

The mutton-chopped man shrugs his shoulders. "We're stuck," he says. "Should just be a minute."

"We don't have a minute," I bark.

Rose leans in the direction of the sculpture, across my body. "How's it know my name?"

"Driver!"

The light turns green, but we are still blocked by the taxi. "Move it," the driver calls out.

"Robert, what's that?"

"I told you, dear, it's a monster. Don't pay it any due."

"But … But …" Rose's voice trails off.

Just then, following a cluster of rapid bursts of light, words form on #*dunamisto*'s screen.

"Your name is Rosemary Caputo, and you were born in South Philadelphia. Other than this trip to New York, you have never left your neighborhood. Your parents both died in an automobile accident when you were six years old, and you were raised by your alcoholic aunt, who died weeks after your twenty-first birthday."

I try to cover Rose's eyes, but she again pushes my hands away. I shiver in empathy, for I did not know that she, too, was orphaned at a young age.

"You work in the accounting department of an inner-city hospital and live paycheck to paycheck. Given your deformed foot, you have struggled to form intimate relationships with men. You are a virgin—a status that causes you shame. In addition, you suffer from low self-esteem, which is the reason you have embraced the steampunk culture, as it gives you a sense of belonging and purpose (although only an imagined one, for your participation cannot hide your loneliness). There is little hope for you."

Rose gasps. Heartbroken, livid, I too gasp at the beast's cruel and gratuitous attack. The cab in front of us turns the corner, opening a path. The driver, the man who comes from some distant time, snaps the reins, and we resume our journey west. I look at Rose, my dearest Rose, who weeps with a pain that I well understand.

"Stop," I scream to the driver. "Stop now!" The driver pulls the reins and brings the carriage to a complete stop in front of the plaza. "Excuse me," I say to Rose. "This assault must not go unavenged. No one—and I mean no one..."

I am enraged, not just at #*dunamisto*, but at my propriety as well—my good manners, my fear of righteous rage, my compulsion toward decency when decency is not deserved. I think of the sassy woman on the courthouse steps.

"No one," I declare, "no one fucks with my girl."

I leap from the carriage and stand before #*dunamisto*. I look up to the monstrosity, to this great inverted *Y*. I believe that it winks at me with a hint of condescension, with a hint of malignant satisfaction at having decimated not just a man, but the woman he loves. My rage grows in volcanic fashion and, defiant, I step forward. I shake my fist at its deathly mass, at the colossal monitor by its side. In the distance, I hear the wails of my dear Rose—and I turn to see that the driver (this anachronistic man whom I admire) comforts my love in the most chivalrous way. *Good man!*

I look around the plaza and see that a crowd is gathering, and I wonder if these curious people anticipate some sort of duel between this monstrosity and me. Rising from this otherwise anonymous crowd, I see the panama hat so familiar to me—and the head and body beneath it. Polsky! I smirk with grim satisfaction, for the ever-irritating professor has arrived at the most opportune moment.

I recall #*dunamisto*'s final, icy words directed at Rose: "There is little hope for you." I stomp in rage toward the sculpture and stop just feet away. I take a deep breath and gather my strength, the moral outrage that I have long felt but have been loath to discharge. I consider my father's heroism on the battlefield—his Medal of Honor, his Purple Heart. "No matter how hard you try, you can never be your father—and you will always be your mother."

"*#dunamisto*," I howl, "your time has come! The time when I, on behalf of many, tell you what *you* are."

"Robert Walser," the thing interrupts with a flash on the screen.

"Don't you dare." I shake my fist. "Don't you fucking dare!" The screen turns black, empty. "I believe that I've earned the right to turn the cold lens of examination on you," I continue.

"So here is who you are. *What* you are. You are nothing more than a ... Actually, let's start with what you're not. That's easier. You're not *art*, as that would require some inspiration—some *spontaneous* inspiration—some ethos, some transmission of feeling. And if you think that creating a psychic wound is the transmission of feeling ... attacking a poor woman because of her deformity ... if you think that what you do is the transmission of feeling in the spirit of art, then you are sadly mistaken. For to elicit a negative feeling as the result of cruelty is different than to elicit a negative emotion from empathy, from identification, from shared suffering. The latter is transcendent, the former base. And nothing, of course, compares to the transmission of some exaltation, some joy, some giddiness in the soul. No, sir, no. You are none of these things. You do none of these things. No. No. You are nothing more than an amalgamation, a conglomeration ... a hodgepodge of nuts and bolts, wires and silica, fiberglass and metal. A slave to three masters: commerce, military, the arts. A sickening troika.

"Who are you, *#dunamisto*? And who is your one true master? Each work of art must have one true master, you know. One man, one woman, one child. *Someone*. Others can be involved, of course, and rare is the work of art that has been touched by only one human being. But who is your master? Is it some army general? Some lieutenant? Some nameless captain of industry? A technologist? A programmer? Perhaps you have many masters, many masters with some interests competing and some aligned.

"But I am not fooled, for it is the alignment of your masters' interests, rather than the conflict, that frightens me most—for what could your three masters possibly have in common? On what sacred ground could they possibly unite? What good could come of their twisted collaboration? And as you are a product of this collaboration, the birth of their collaboration, the *after*-birth, my question has been answered. You, sir, are a monstrosity, as is your triad of creators. A mutant, not with a brain but with merely a representation of a brain, one that does nothing more than aggregate data under the guise of original thought. An algorithm that lacks the most essential quality—compassion. A soulless beast that finds glee in the malice of its programmers, a dark cadre of socially awkward engineers, outsiders who revel in their new-found potency and who use this potency for malignant purposes. An accumulator of information that has no idea how to use this accumulated information for the good of our great people.

"You collect and collect and collect with the belief that more is better, determining the proper use of this data, the most expedient use, only after it has been acquired. Testing, dabbling, experimenting until some value—real or perceived—is unlocked. Making misstep after misstep without even the faintest apology. For everything is done, you say, in furtherance of some vague and elusive advancement—an advancement that you are convinced is understood better by you and your masters than by me or Rose or the mutton-chopped driver.

"And in your piousness, in your hallucinogenic micro-dosing of god knows what, you wrap yourself in such a vague and righteous cloak that you are impenetrable, immune to criticism, for to question you—to question your masters—is to question God himself. Or so you say. And because to question God is a fool's errand, you think you have won. But rest assured, you have not!"

I shake my fist at the sculpture's mutated head and scan the plaza, which is now filled with hundreds of people—all quiet, all listening. I am encircled by the crowd, which appears to unite in its disdain for *#dunamisto*. I notice that Polsky has made his way to the front row, and he stares at me as if he is reassessing his view of me, and perhaps my father. I turn to look at Rose. With the help of the driver, she disembarks from the carriage. She takes an unsure step down to the pavement, gathers herself, and then hobbles toward me. She walks with the greatest dignity—the dignity of the humble soul.

I turn back to *#dunamisto* and make a decision. I dart behind the large monitor and grab the cable, which is connected to a nearby power source. In an effort to disable this beast, to render it impotent, I pull at the cable, attempting to dislodge it. I struggle to remove the stubborn cord and fear that I may fail, that this monster shall prevail, that Rose—and Polsky, too—will witness my failure. But just as I am about to surrender, another hand appears on the cable, and then a second. I look up to see that these hands belong to none other than the plump Iowan, Helen Schweitzer! She pants furiously, her fingers tight, her brow twisted in determination. She pulls the cable, adding her strength, one fueled by her outrage, by her hunger for revenge and for what is right. Our fury united, we pull as one, our bodies angled together. Within seconds, the head of the cable snaps from the monitor, and a flurry of sparks indicates that we have wounded this monster. The crowd cheers, erupting in a primal glee.

I step back, look up to the monitor, and see that it is black. There are no words, no colors, no lights. The fine Helen Schweitzer—God bless her—gives me a warm Midwestern hug and disappears into the crowd.

The throng now migrates toward *#dunamisto*. The horde's movement, its sheer power, makes me worried for Rose's wellbeing. I search for her and, after a few frightening seconds, am relieved to see her limping in my direction. I push through the mass of people and reach my love. We fall into the most desperate embrace.

"Thanks," she whispers. "Thanks for fightin' for me."

As if we are dance partners, we spin in the midst of the throng, and as we rotate I notice that several people have climbed atop *#dunamisto*. They sit on its sloped shoulders, on its twisted head. A young man tears the panel from the sculpture and proceeds to rip the entrails—wires, switches, and cables—from the dark cavity. A few wisps of smoke rise from the hole, and it appears to me that the shoulders of this thing slump in defeat. I lead Rose back to the carriage, careful to protect her from the surrounding chaos. I guide her up into the carriage and, once she is settled, join her on the leather bench.

"Westward," I say to the driver, who snaps the reins dutifully.

I look back to the plaza and see that Polsky gazes at me, his posture erect. He removes his panama hat and places it over his heart. He bows deeply—to me and, I believe, to my father. I tip my cap to him, our equality at last established, even proven. I think of my father, the great Kingsley Walser. I recall the failed boxing lessons he gave me, when my arms flailed, when it became clear to both of us that I lacked the tools necessary to survive in this brutal world. Thick smoke pours from *#dunamisto*, and I know that my father is now watching, that he is proud. I too am proud, for I have at last thrown a punch—and I have connected.

The carriage moves easily down 72nd Street toward the river. The sky is a pearly, opalescent lavender, and the great river below is smooth, placid. A cloud—one single wisp of fluffy white—wafts slow and high like a parade float or a dirigible. Rose holds my hand. And I hold hers. The driver removes his top hat and places it on the seat beside him. I inhale the horse's musky sweat. I listen to the sound of the hooves on the pavement, hypnotized by the rhythm, the cadence, the ease. *Clippity-clop. Clippity-clop.* I kiss Rose on the cheek. She smiles.

As we move forward, I turn and notice a sign on the shop that sells papaya juice and hot dogs. *Help Wanted*, it says. I think about my dire financial situation. I think about the many people who love the shop's combination of sweet and savory, about the joy they experience—and, my snobbery at last surrendered, I vow to apply for that job, to get that job, and, with gratitude, to *do* that job to the very best of my ability.

Clippity-clop. Clippity-clop.

I taste the bitter smoke that pours from *#dunamisto*. Rather than look back at this dying monster, I raise my hand and wave goodbye to the anguish behind me.

Clippity-clop. Clippity-clop.

Rose squeezes my hand. I feel alive.

Today, I *am* alive.